Books by Herbert Tarr

*The Conversion of Chaplain Cohen*
*Heaven Help Us!*
*A Time for Loving*

# A
# TIME FOR
# LOVING

# A
# TIME FOR
# LOVING

## HERBERT TARR

**RANDOM HOUSE     NEW YORK**

Library of Congress Cataloging in Publication Data

Tarr, Herbert.
  A time for loving.

  I. Title.
PZ4.T1786Ti    [PS3570.A65]    813'.5'4    72-2733
ISBN 0-394-46158-4

Manufactured in the United States of America

First Edition

For ANNA and ISIDORE TARGOVNIK

for making it easy for me
to observe the Fifth Commandment

Solomon the King wrote *Song of Songs, Proverbs* and *Ecclesiastes*—in that order. For it is the way of the world:

¶ When a man is young,
he composes songs of love.
¶ When he advances in years,
he expresses his wisdom in maxims and aphorisms.
¶ When he grows old,
he decries the futility of things.

THE MIDRASH

# SOLOMON

He had seen it happen to others. They reached a certain age, or a parent's death left them exposed to the beyond, and they began to unravel. Their hearts dried up like potsherds, their strength melted like wax, they poured out like water. Nothing enticed them any more, neither justice nor power nor fame nor wealth nor love. In the morning they said, "If only it were evening!" and in the evening they said, "If only it were morning!" Dread stalking them by day and fears at night, they raged at themselves and at everyone around them. Yet they could not explain why.

*Was this now befalling him?*

3

Assailed by chills and pains, tightness in the chest and pressure in the head, they withdrew into themselves. They wanted to be alone, but feared loneliness; they sought out people, only to shrink from them. Often they behaved with unforgivable arrogance, before being overcome by emptiness, futility, vanity. And then they wept aloud. Mature men, with wives and many children.

*How could Solomon the King be so afflicted!*

Ruler over all the kingdoms from the Euphrates River to the land of the Philistines and to Egypt, he had established peace from Dan to Beersheba, at last enabling every Israelite to dwell in safety under his vine and under his fig tree. With a now mightily fortified Israel straddling all land routes between Egypt and Arabia and Syria, the King controlled the trade between them and profited greatly from selling Egyptian chariots to Syria and Syrian horses to Egypt. Whereas David his shepherd father knew so little about weaponry that he had burned captured chariots and hamstrung their horses, Solomon's army included fourteen hundred chariots, forty thousand horses and twelve thousand horsemen, housed in special chariot cities built for the King by the same Phoenician stonemasons who had constructed the Palace and the Temple of the Lord.

Solomon so surpassed the kings of the earth that all his drinking vessels were of gold, silver counted as nothing in Jerusalem, and all peoples sought his presence. After observing the King, his palace compound, repasts, servants, richly appareled retinue, the sacrifices offered at the Temple, the Queen of Sheba exclaimed, "The half of it was not told me! Your wisdom and prosperity exceed the reports I had heard. Praised be the Lord your God, who delighted in setting you on Israel's throne. Because the Lord loved Israel, He made you King."

*Why, then, did Solomon no longer* feel *like King?*

Here was a riddle worthy of Solomon: How could the wisest man under the sun be double-minded, distracted, unable to concentrate on anything long enough to consummate it? He saw life slipping away and himself powerless to hold it fast. Only hope could save the King, but he had none. Was he, perhaps, losing his reason?

Beside him now in bed lay an inert body. He didn't care whose; heat and rest concerned him more, for lately he found it as impossible to keep warm as to sleep through the night. And what did the names of his harem matter, when their substance was interchangeable? Women fell into two types: deep ditches or narrow pits, who were snares and traps; and the fretfully contentious, much like a continual dropping on a very rainy day. How their conversations brightened when illuminated by flashes of silence.

From the look of the soiled coverlet, this night's companion was Rainbow. Coated from head to sole with all the dyes of the East, she always appeared in so many hues that nobody recalled her original color, or whether she had any.

He uncovered her. Behold Rainbow: hennaed palms and soles, finger- and toenails, carmined breasts with a sachet of myrrh between them, kohl-blackened eyes, yellow hair, rouged cheeks, and pink lips which had nibbled him to sleep. Alas, her own sleep was the exhausted one of the overworked but underused.

Rainbow stirred, smearing her paints across the bed. Soon she would awaken—a chilling prospect, for she would talk. Why were women's conversations like labyrinths, from which they never emerged with sense intact and he never able to penetrate? At the first opening he would have to anchor a thought, then unwind it like a ball of thread to serve as guide through all their bewildering chatterings. Men knew that death and life are in the power of the tongue; women used it as yet another sexual appendage.

"Again, my lord?" Awake now, Rainbow offered herself to him like foodstuff.

But how could the King repeat what he had not yet done? Once Solomon had an eye and more for every desirable female; these past weeks an eye was all he could muster. Once! Is there a sadder word in any language?

A clap of the hands summoned guards to remove the single-minded Rainbow. Then Solomon sent for his physician, who would prescribe more worthless poultices of hot moist figs and dips in the sacred Jordan or the warm baths beyond the river. No matter. The only medicine for the lonely eeriness of the night was company.

Solomon had left Jerusalem a few days before, because as one's prosperity grows, so does the number of people who consume it. While the poor are hated even by their own neighbors, he reflected wryly, the rich have multitudes of friends. Thousands ate at the King's table daily: the harem, priests, government officials, courtiers, royal guard, soldiers, court musicians, Levites, administrators—all devout observers of the Lord's first commandment: Be fruitful and multiply.

That afternoon the King had come to Ezion-

Geber at the Gulf of Aqabah on the shore of the Red
Sea to tour his smeltery, where the copper ore dug in
Sinai was refined, then manufactured into all kinds
of bronze articles, from fishhooks and plowshares to
weapons. These, Solomon's navy carried to the four
corners of the earth in exchange for gold, also silver,
ivory, apes, peacocks. The only one like it in the
world, his copper refinery reassured Solomon that
indeed he was unlike other men.

Upon arrival, then, what made him shut himself
inside his chamber in dread? Consider his other
achievements. By dividing the land into twelve well-
administered districts without regard to old tribal
boundaries, Solomon had at last organized the former
self-governing tribes into one nation. No more indif-
ference to a brother tribe under enemy attack, no
further antagonism between the North's ten tribes
and the South's Judah. Israel was now united, its
strength multiplied twelvefold.

David's once simple agricultural land Solomon
had turned into a commercial and industrial state
that eclipsed Egypt and Assyria. Each Israelite district conscripted workmen four months every year for
industry and construction, donated very substantial
taxes to the treasury, and forwarded in turn one

month's provisions for the royal court. Except Judah, because the King and his retinue lived in Jerusalem.

Solomon's Jerusalem, center of the world! Surely the Lord Himself drew joy and vitality from the palace compound, so sumptuous it had taken thirteen years to construct. The adjacent Temple attested that the Lord dwelt in the King's own house and smiled on him. So did the pharaoh's daughter, Solomon's chief wife, the first Egyptian princess given in marriage to a foreigner. Isis' dowry was the city of Gezer and an alliance of peace with her father. The Israelites had fled Egypt as slaves; now Israel was Egypt's superior.

When the chief Queen failed to give him an heir, Solomon had appointed his eldest son his successor in order to obviate the murderous battles for the throne such as had plagued Saul and David. Everything calculated to ensure the monarchy's peaceful continuity. For peace, of course, was Solomon's greatest attainment. In addition to glory and majesty, he had given the Israelites forty years of rest and quietness. No wonder Israel's population had doubled during his reign.

*Then why did Solomon fear?*

"My lord."

The elderly physician had arrived, his reputation

secured by his own longevity. No eighty-year-old could be a bad doctor, even if he prescribed bone dust and rancid fat mixed with animal offal.

"My lord still feels cold?" he asked.

"Cold?" He wanted to reveal his sense of sorrow and foreboding. But why invite comparison with Israel's first king, who went mad? Voicing his feelings might translate them into reality, which could then overpower him. "Yes, I still feel cold."

The physician lay a pillow of hot stones at Solomon's feet, saying, "My lord must remember that cold is age's warmest friend."

Wordplay the King appreciated as the foreplay of minds. "Another such proverb," he jested, "and punishment shall be your reward."

"I try my best; I accomplish what's possible. My lord must learn to do likewise."

"The possible is for commoners; kings require more. Why can't I warm myself?"

"Everyone wishes to live long," said the physician with a sigh, "but nobody wants to grow old."

Solomon frowned. "You say I am old?"

"Of course not, certainly not. My lord has never looked younger."

"When people start praising your youthfulness," the King observed, "it's a sure sign you've aged. But why does my blood freeze at fifty-five, when David lived till seventy?"

"Your father lived a more vigorous life. David was a soldier all his days, his life one continuous battle."

Solomon's temper flared. "Uniting a kingdom and fortifying it, setting up trade treaties and alliances, building a navy and chariot cities and industries—that you don't call a vigorous life! My father left me a mountain fortress of thirteen acres, the City of David; I created Jerusalem. A mule carried me to be anointed; my son Rehoboam shall ride in a horse-drawn chariot. I inherited disorganized tribes with nomadic ways"—a sudden breeze chilled him—"and a back that's a prickling pillar of ice. I remember—" He broke off.

"Yes, my lord?"

Solomon touched his feet to the pillow of hot stones. "When David was stricken with years, he too couldn't keep warm. Presently he was gathered to his fathers."

The physician said, "I remember prescribing a comely young virgin to warm David."

Abishag from Shunem, whom Solomon had inherited with the throne. His older brother, Adonijah, had tried to depose Solomon by marrying her, David's widow, and instead achieved his own execution. "The Shunemite never helped my father. He never knew her."

"He was seventy years old then. You're only fifty-five, the perfect age for knowing young virgins."

"Forty years of advance in government, commerce, industry, religion, art, wisdom—and my physician still prescribes hot stones and young virgins!" With a gesture he dismissed the physician. What medicine, after all, could inflame ice, or stay the loss of all sensuous delight? Now all women looked alike to him, alas, music no longer sounded the same, wine had turned to wormwood, and his gardens at Etam appeared drab. Even his fine linen raiment reminded him of sackcloth, and food tasted like ashes.

*Whom was he mourning?*

No matter: life's story had but one ending. What mattered in the meantime was that *nothing* mattered any more. Yet how long could a man live on nothing?

"Vanity of vanities," Solomon cried aloud, "all is vanity! What does a man gain from all his toil beneath the sun? One generation passes away and another arises, but the earth abides forever, unchanged. The sun rises and the sun sets, then hastens to rise again. The wind circles continuously, always returning to its rounds. All the rivers flow into the sea, but the sea is never full . . . All things are wearisome beyond words; the eye is never satisfied with seeing, nor the ear filled with hearing. Only what has been will be, and what has been done will be done again. There is nothing new under the sun."

If, Solomon mused, despair assaulted a king, who had everything, it probably lay waste a host of commoners, who had little. But alas, one's soul must indeed be cast down if he looks to the misery of others for comfort.

A knock at the door.

"Your son Rehoboam," said a guard. "He asks to see you."

"At midnight?"

A thin, flutelike voice piped through the door, "I noticed your physician leave, Father."

Rather, the physician had gone to the Prince and told him to cheer his father: forty years before, the physician had dispatched Solomon to David on the same errand. But what different messengers! Had Moses, speculated the King, led the nomadic Hebrews to Canaan to conquer it under Joshua, whereupon each tribe went its separate way under the sporadic leadership of local warrior-judges until a century of enemy attacks made the Israelites compel Samuel

13

the prophet to unify them under the kingship of Saul
—only to end up with *Rehoboam?* Incredible!

"Send him in," Solomon said. In the middle of
a sleepless night the Prince was more welcome than
nobody.

Rehoboam crept into the chamber, a shadow cast
by Solomon—a shadow that was now stalking him.
The Prince with the frozen smile looked smaller and
thinner than ever, as if anxiety for the crown were
gradually swallowing him. Beware anyone, thought
the King, whose smile never reaches his eyes and
whose eyes flee yours. Such a man blesses with his
mouth but curses inwardly.

"How *are* you, Father?"

"Vitally concerned, aren't you?"

"Certainly, Father. How I feel depends on how
you feel." That Solomon believed. "That's why I
followed you to Ezion-Geber. The way you've been
acting lately. Are you ill?"

"Ill—me? On the contrary. I'm planning to rule
another forty years. How do you feel?"

Rehoboam's smile dissolved. "Terrible."

"Oh? You looked fine when you entered."

"Did I? Well, I try to look my best so you
shouldn't worry about my health as I do about yours."

If only Jeroboam, commander of the levy of

laborers in the North, could have been Solomon's successor. How splendidly he had overseen the building
of Jerusalem's walls. What a superb monarch he
would make. The King loved Jeroboam like a son—
except, of course, he despised his son. Had it been
wise for Solomon to make the throne hereditary and
to appoint Rehoboam his successor?

"Father?"

"Yes?"

"I was thinking," Rehoboam began, and Solomon refrained from saying, "Good, that's an improve-
ment," because what was coming would be the only
thought his son ever had. Awaken the Prince in the
middle of the day, and he'd say, as he did now, "You
were very young when you ascended the throne,
weren't you? Fifteen."

"My father died when I was fifteen. You aren't
that fortunate. Why look so shocked? Every son wants
his father dead so he can become his own master.
Ask your sons."

"My sons feel toward me as I do toward you?"
Solomon nodded.

"How—wonderful. I am—overjoyed."

The King smiled.

"Still, David made you co-regent during his lifetime."

"He was on his deathbed." A fleeting memory of his father dying while his mother busied herself with securing the royal succession for Solomon, who did not have first claim to the throne. "Nobody relinquishes power, Rehoboam. It always relinquishes him."

"But I'm nearly forty years old and still only Prince. So humiliating."

"Forty? A pity. After forty, everything is regrets."

"Oh, that's very *good*, Father. A new proverb?"

Solomon scrutinized his son in sad wonder. "God grants a man riches, property, honor—everything he can possibly desire. Yet how can he enjoy it all, knowing some stranger will consume it!"

"Stranger? I am bone of your bones and flesh of your flesh."

"Yes," said the King ruefully, "your mother was so faithful."

"Well, then? Will you appoint me co-regent, as David appointed you?"

Fury gripped Solomon. "I told you, David was *dying*," he shouted. "Do you know what death is, Rehoboam? What strikes down everyone else, you think now. Well, wait, my son, *wait*." All at once the King realized when sorrow had first visited him. It started the month before, with Rehoboam's first mention of a co-regency. Had Solomon, then, been mourning the loss of his own self? "This discussion is ended. You may go."

Rehoboam did not move. "Are you sure you want to be alone?"

"What do you think I am when you're here?"

"If you are ill, Father—"

"*Out!*"

The Prince departed without his smile, and Solomon burrowed into bed and tried not to think of his son. With Rehoboam co-regent, what would that make Solomon? Awaiting burial.

If only he could fall asleep now without dreaming. He couldn't remember his recent dreams, only that they often startled him awake. Once he had loved dreams more than lovemaking. Another once. In his first dream as monarch, the Lord appeared to the fifteen-year-old, saying, "Ask—what shall I give you?"

"I am only a child," he had replied, "hardly knowing how to go out and come in. Yet now I am the King of a great people. Give Your servant therefore an understanding heart, that I may discern between good and evil."

His request pleased the Lord. "Because you did

not ask for long life, nor for riches nor honor nor the life of your enemies, but instead requested wisdom and knowledge to judge My people, unparalleled wisdom and honor are granted you. I shall also give you incomparable riches and glory. And if you will walk in My ways and keep My Law, as your father David did, then I will lengthen your days."

All had been fulfilled beyond measure—the wisdom and the honor, the riches and the glory. All except the most vital, without which everything else was worthless.

"O Lord, now I do beseech You," he cried aloud. "Lengthen my days. Lord?"

Silence.

"Do not hide Your face from me!"

No answer.

"*Lord!* For David's sake, turn not away from Your anointed."

Not even an echo.

David had often said, "If you seek God, He will be found." *Where?* Now Solomon swung between faith in the Lord and despair, from the old world of certainty to unbelief. Only a prophet or a fool was capable of believing anything any more—and the King still wondered whether it was wiser to believe too much or too little.

What if he were to appeal to *gods?* Would they respond, those idols his foreign wives worshiped in the alien shrines Solomon had built them atop the Mount of Olives? Or might the Lord God strike him down for whoring?

His father had trusted utterly in the Lord. A shepherd, David could worship God in a sanctuary that was a tent and cavort before the Holy Ark in public. Born to the purple, Solomon dignified the worship of God by constructing the resplendent Temple, though His essence always eluded him. Foreign deities could at least be defined, though anything defined was thereby diminished.

The King recalled David's dying charge. "I am now, my son, going to my destiny. I must depart to my fathers and travel the common road of all men, now alive or yet to be, from which no one can ever return to learn what is happening among the living . . . I exhort you to be just toward your subjects and pious toward God, and to keep His commandments. Do not neglect them by yielding to favor or flattery or lust or any other passion . . . I go the way of all the earth. Be strong, Solomon, and show yourself a man."

Certainly hundreds of wives and concubines and women had proved Solomon's manhood, and his policies of taxation and forced labor had established the monarchy as an everlasting power, which would ensure peace forever.

"Then, *why*, O Lord!"

Why had Solomon never attained peace within himself? With all his wisdom he could not understand. Nor why the Israelites did not love him as they still loved David. Forty years gone and still their beloved, as Solomon would never be if he lived till one hundred and twenty.

True, the tribal elders had elected his father King, while Solomon was appointed by David, and there was more romance in a shepherd ascending the throne than a prince. But David was a man of blood, who warred continually to establish the nation; why did the people remember him best as "the sweet singer of Israel"? Even after his adultery with Bathsheba and her husband Uriah's murder, even after Nathan the prophet's condemnation, "You are the man, the adulterer and murderer"—Israel loved David still.

But not David's own sons. Amnon the incestuous rapist, Absalom the fratricide and would-be patricide, Adonijah the usurper, all proved David a poor master of his own household. (Yet this endeared him still more to the people! Who has not fathered an ungrateful child?) Solomon, born of David's old age into

Bathsheba's intrigues, regarded his father as a life-
line. For everyone knew that the anointment of a new
king coincided with the funerals of all his brothers.

David's final words Solomon would never forget,
nor fully believe. "Remember, my son: God rules
man, but the righteous rule God. He may make
decrees, but the righteous may annul them with
prayer."

Memories, the older the clearer. Like winter
snows that topped Mount Lebanon into summer, they
capped all Solomon's thoughts of late. Slowly memory
was replacing hope, alas, just as apathy had conquered
all desire.

He drifted off to sleep . . .

. . . *inside a pagan temple . . . something long
and thin crawls out of the mouth of a statue . . . a
silver scroll with a beautifully inscribed message in a
strange language . . . even his foreign wives and concubines cannot decipher it . . .*

*The scroll reads itself aloud: "I, Shadad ben
Adad, sovereign over a thousandthousand provinces
. . . rode on a thousandthousand horses . . . ruled
over a thousandthousand kings . . . slew a thousandthousand warriors . . . Yet when the Angel of Death
approached me . . . I could not prevail."*

*He flings the scroll to the earth . . . It turns into*

*a worm and inches toward him . . . He cuts off its head . . . It still advances . . . He tries to flee . . . His legs will not move . . . The headless worm gnaws at him . . . He crumbles to dust . . . Nothing is left visible . . . but his crown . . .*

Solomon struggled to open his eyes; they remained closed. He cried out; no sound was heard. All the while his heart beat at his ribs, trying to break out. He gasped for air; there was none. He dug his nails into the palms of his hands until pain finally forced him awake. Swimming then in cold sweat, the King treaded panic.

At last he knew what terrified him. It had a name. The grave. The Lord may have been David's shepherd; Solomon's was death.


At dawn the King fled Ezion-Geber for Jerusalem.

# SHULAMITH

*D*od!

He came springing from the mountains and skipping over the hills, like a hart. Now he stood behind the house and peered through the lattice, calling:

"Arise, my love, my fair one, and come away. For lo, the winter is past, the rains are over and gone. Flowers bedeck the earth, the time of singing is come, and the voice of the turtledove is heard in our land. The fig tree sweetens her green fruits, the blossoming vines exhale their fragrance. Arise, my love, my fair one, and come away!"

She hesitated, and he implored:

"O my dove, show me your face, let me hear your voice, for your voice is sweet and you are comely . . ."

She rushed outside and seized him, would not let him go till she had brought him within.

He kissed her. "Your lips, Shulamith, drop sweetness. Honey and milk are under your tongue."

Shy, she pulled away.

"A closed garden is my Shulamith," he teased, "a fountain sealed."

"Not so! I am a well of living waters." She drew him down beside her. "Blow upon my garden, make its perfumes flow . . . Let my love enter his garden and eat its fruit."

They intertwined.

"I am come into my garden, my bride . . . I pluck my myrrh and spices . . . I lick honey from the comb."

"Eat, my Dod . . . drink my love . . ."

Awakening, Shulamith kept her eyes shut. Sleep allowed the seventeen-year-old what she denied herself awake. She knew too intimately the emptiness that awaited her in the windowless hut, with her two brothers away tending sheep and Dod again conscripted.

Where was he now? In Lebanon felling cedars, or floating them down the Great Sea to Joppa, or hauling them overland to Jerusalem, which Solomon had been adorning for forty years? Did Dod dream of her as she constantly dreamed of him? Or did he dream instead of Solomon? At times the King's policies seemed to enrage the shepherd more than Shulamith delighted him. Recently Dod even espoused rebellion, the ten Northern tribes against the South's Judah. Yet this was the same nineteen-year-old who apologized to lambs when he sheared them.

The sound of rainwater leaking into the hut finally roused Shulamith. Swiftly she disentangled her cloak from her arms and legs, then ran to unbolt the door and let in the light.

"Praise God!" Spring, routing winter with the suddenness of the sun shooting up out of the Jordan Valley, had splashed scarlet wildflowers across the Plain of Esdraelon, like drops of blood. "Praise God for restoring the earth to life."

Shulamith donned her homespun mantle of black goathair and climbed the outside stairs to the roof. This house, outside the village of Shunem, she had helped to build, kneading the clay with water, finely chopped straw, and small stones, then pressing

27

the mixture into a portable wooden mold. Three days of summer sun had baked the bricks dry, but after downpours the roof had to be smoothed with a roller, lest the house revert to earth. Sometimes it made the girl feel she lived in a grave.

But not today. Blooming pomegranate trees had turned the hillside a fiery coral, and blue finches nuzzled drifts of white Stars of Bethlehem in the green pastureland that extended north to the hills of Galilee and Mount Hermon. From afar its snowy peak shimmered like a giant almond blossom, spring's first sign of life to come.

Before her stretched Jacob's deathbed blessing fulfilled: the tribe of Issachar's land sprawled like a large-boned ass, sunning itself lazily among the pleasant hills. With springs that winter could not freeze nor summer dry, plenty of space here for people and flocks, for greenery and flowers, for lolling and loving. Here warrior-judges Deborah and Gideon had vanquished the Canaanite and Midianite oppressors. Later, when the Philistines slew King Saul and Prince Jonathan upon the heights, David had won back the land, after lamenting, "How anguished am I, my brother Jonathan. You were so dear to me, and wondrous your love, surpassing the love of women. How are the mighty fallen!"

28

Would anyone ever love Shulamith so? Of course: Dod. But though they felt like two profiles of the same face, he had as much chance of marrying her as an Israelite girl did Solomon. The King loved many women—seven hundred wives and three hundred concubines from Egypt, Moab, Ammon, Edom, Zidon and other lands—all foreigners with whom the Lord had forbidden any kind of intercourse lest they seduce Israel to worship their alien gods. Still, Shulamith considered Solomon the umbilical cord that bound the Lord God to His people.

"Exactly so," Dod had commented. "And you know what must be done to the umbilical cord to enable children to live and grow." He always raged at any mention of the King, as if Solomon were not Israel's ruler, but destroyer. Forced labor and the taxes exacted to support Solomon's endless construction and huge harem had embittered Dod.

Not Shulamith's father, however, though he remained too poor to afford another bride-price after her mother's death in childbirth. Without a murmur he accepted life's six beastly stages following the first joyous one: "At one year of age, man is a king, deferred to and embraced. At two a pig, he gropes in the gutters; at ten he skips like a goat; at twenty he neighs like a horse as he seeks a wife. After marriage he bears his burdens like an ass and hardens his face like a dog in search of sustenance. In old age he becomes an ape, halfway back from being human."

Her father also taught happier things. That love is deeds, not feelings; beauty is acts, not appearance; whoever loves silver will never be satisfied with silver; rich is whoever is content with his lot; sweet is the slumber of the laboring man, even if he has little to eat, for the rich man's abundance does not let him sleep for worrying. (Asa had remarked, "Give me the riches and I'll take the worries." And Ben responded, "I fear we'll both have to settle for half your wish.")

On his deathbed he had begged forgiveness for a father's task unconcluded, for leaving Shulamith unwed. During his last months on earth, he confessed, selfishness made him keep her close to him. She told of discouraging suitors, because none was good enough to be his son-in-law, and her father replied, "A considerate lie is also love," and died smiling. How she missed him. Surely the Lord, Himself One, would not keep them apart forever.

After the roof was smoothed, Shulamith descended to count stones in a jar. They confirmed that Dod's four months' forced labor for that year had ended, unless he had stumbled over his own tongue. Government officers would not enjoy hearing conscription called Solomonic bondage.

Now she set about baking cakes of barley. Shunem grew the best wheat in all Israel, but only those as rich as her piggish cousin Mushi could afford that luxury. Kneeling in the yard, the girl crushed barley with a pestle and mortar, kneading it with water and salt in a wooden mixing bowl, and leavened it with a fermented lump from the previous day's baking. She placed thin cakes of the barley mixture upon an inverted shallow bowl that half covered a small fire, then prepared a stew of lentils and beans flavored with coriander and black cumin.

Next, the vineyard. Her brothers had assigned her to it instead of the flocks in order to separate her from Dod. The sun might accomplish that, she feared, for it had burned her skin almost as black as her hair, and soon no man could tell her from her goats. A headcloth shading her face, Shulamith hurried up the hill.

As she pruned away weak branches in order to drive their strength into the main ones, she sang, "Catch us the foxes, the little foxes, that ruin our vineyards . . ." She trimmed the branches close to their stumps, leaving no more than three feet of vines. "Catch us the foxes, the little foxes, for our vines have tender grapes . . ."

Afterward she rested under a fig tree to eat carob pods and daydream of Dod. With his ruddy complexion and curly black hair, bearded cheeks like beds of spices, arms of rounded gold, legs like marble pillars, a mouth filled with sweetness, he was altogether made for love.

"Shulamith? Shulamith?"

Her heart skipped. Dod? Instead she saw a stranger below in front of the hut. He was unloading a giant bouquet of purples, scarlets, reds, and yellows.

He motioned to her.

Warily she descended toward a display of many colors, all tunics and jewelry. Enough there to outfit Solomon's harem.

The stranger, in ornamented fine linen, bowed low when she approached. "Ornan of Megiddo, dresser of the fairest and wealthiest. Of you too, I hope—" Raising his eyes as she pushed back her headcloth, his mouth fell open. "As the Lord lives!"

"What's the matter?"

"You are the most beautiful girl I have ever seen!"

Shulamith expressed no thanks. Beautiful, she

knew, is what men call virgins until they can call them harlot.

Recovering, Ornan said, "No more coarse sackcloth for you. Nor wool—that's for commoners. For you only the finest linen from Egypt will do." He held up each tunic, then spread before her all manner of jewelry and sandals, a mirror of polished bronze, tweezers, ear-picks and a bronze razor, also seashells containing six different colors for beautifying the face and body.

A presentation fit for Isis. "Why show me all this?"

"Choose what you want. Not that beauty such as yours can be enhanced. All it needs is to be seen. Well, which will you take?"

Shulamith laughed. "Everything."

"A wise choice." The merchant mounted his mule. "Your brothers may pay me on the day of your betrothal."

"Wait! Asa and Ben can't afford so much as a single earring."

"They haven't told you yet?" said Ornan as he rode off. "Your cousin Mushi has asked to marry you, and your brothers have accepted."

\* \* \*

Shulamith did not stop running till she had confronted Ben and Asa in the field amid their flocks.

"I hate Mushi! I despise Mushi! I loathe Mushi!"

Twenty-year-old Asa shrugged. "Mushi is our cousin, hence our equal in every respect. Except, of course, money."

"Mushi already has a wife."

"He has *two* wives," boasted Asa. "And two concubines. You'll be the envy of all Shunem, marrying a man who can afford so many women. And the housework will be divided five ways."

Her favorite brother, twenty-four-year-old Ben, spoke up. "The Law commands us to contract your marriage. You know that, Shulamith. Just as the Law obligates you to heed tradition."

"*Why* must I heed tradition?"

The question startled both men. Apparently, asking it had violated tradition.

"Tell me why."

"Because tradition requires," Asa replied, "that tradition be kept."

Ben continued, "Since the bride's kinship to both sides ensures respect for her, you know everyone prefers marriage between cousins. Virgins' families ask of kinsmen only half the usual *mohar*."

34

"What good will half a bride-price do the two of you?"

"Happily, Mushi offered us three times the usual *mohar*. But don't think this affected our decision."

Shulamith was half convinced. Money did not influence Ben, she knew, for he had never had any. For the same reason Asa was never swayed by anything *but* money. Two brothers, yet so different. Ben, hard-muscled and upright, had sifted from their father's seed all the wheat, leaving Asa the chaff.

"I am not a sheep to be bought," Shulamith cried. "I am a woman."

Asa chuckled. "We have a little sister who has no breasts, and she calls herself a woman."

"I have so!" She turned red. "I mean, I am. And what I am not, is for sale."

"No Israelite is sold into marriage," Ben exclaimed angrily. "The *mohar* only compensates us for losing you. Nothing degrading about it, especially when the groom offers a bride-price as high as Solomon's for a concubine. It publicly demonstrates Mushi's esteem for you—would any husband mistreat such an investment? What's more, Asa and I will lavish a goodly portion of the *mohar* on you. We've already spoken to a merchant from Megiddo about clothing and jewelry."

"Do you know what we're giving you on your betrothal day?" said Asa. "A headpiece of silver!"

Ben added meaningfully, "If she's been a wall."

"Of course. If she's been a door," warned Asa, "we would have to board her up in cedarwood."

What did that mean? The Law called for the death of any bride found not to be a virgin. "I *am* a wall." (Else she would not keep dreaming of swinging like a gate.)

"You'd better be." Asa looked worried. "Your virginity is all we have. If you forsake it even once, we'll be forced to keep ours always." Mushi's *mohar*, Shulamith realized, would at last enable Ben and Asa to acquire brides of their own. Land, too. ". . . No longer will we be lowly shepherds," the younger brother exulted. " 'A man who does not own land is not truly a man.' In our case, doubly true; since we don't own land, we haven't been able to possess women."

Ben nodded. " 'A man who has no wife lives without joy, blessing, peace, and good.' "

"Or lovemaking," added Asa. "Not that I mind having so little. It's not having so much that's made me bitter."

36

Ben said quietly, "It doesn't please me, Shula-mith, to appear to be exchanging you for wives and land. But know that our negotiations with Mushi guarantee your good treatment. Don't look at me like that!" He turned away. "It's Solomon's fault. Curse him for keeping us poor. Maybe the North *should* break away from the South—"

"I'd rebel myself," Asa remarked, "but who has the time? Rebellions are for the rich, like Mushi. And why should a rich man rebel?"

Shulamith took a deep breath. "Hear me! I am one wall that Mushi will not climb. Marry a pig, bearded like a goat, with the head of a horse and the sense of an ass, and a jackal for a mouth? *Never.*"

Asa shrugged. "So Mushi is not the handsomest man in Israel. But when a man is rich, everyone considers him a good husband—and good-looking too."

"My husband," declared Shulamith, "will be Dod."

"One of Mushi's shepherds?" said Ben, infuriated. "Dod ben Nobody?"

"Dod, my love." (*He* could vouch for her breasts.)

"A stranger to Shunem, an orphan . . . a landless pauper."

"Dod is as rich as we!"

37

"How can you lie like that?" Asa was outraged. "Ben and I are almost *farmers*."

That evening Shulamith determined to appeal to the King in Jerusalem, every Israelite's right. Surely Solomon would save her, having founded the Temple itself on love. When the King was planning the House of God, a heavenly voice directed him to a field on Mount Zion owned by two brothers—one a poor bachelor, the other a wealthy married man with many children. It was harvest time, and the poor brother had secretly added his own heaps of grain to the rich one's, feeling his large family needed extra food. Meanwhile, the rich brother was secretly shifting his grain to the poor brother's store. These acts of love inspired Solomon to buy the brothers' field for the Temple site. Surely such a man would bless her love for Dod.

Afraid to await Dod's return, for her brothers had decided to advance the betrothal date, Shulamith spent a sleepless night. Why was she being tormented, she who had never harmed anyone?

When asked why misfortune more often strikes good people than bad, her father had replied, "If a man has two cows, one strong and the other weak, which one does he work hard? The strong one, of course. So the Lord doesn't test the wicked, because they couldn't stand the trial. Whom then does he try? The righteous." Shulamith expressed doubt, and he continued, "Look. When a potter tests his furnace, he doesn't test it with cracked jars, because a single blow would break them. Isn't that so? Instead he tests with sound jars, which can withstand many knocks."

Now the girl prayed for a journey without tests and a life without Mushi.

Until dawn Shulamith comforted herself with tales of the City of David, which comprised nine of the ten measures of beauty that the Lord God had bestowed upon the world. Creation had begun at Zion, the center of the earth, which nourished the entire world. At Jerusalem heaven was joined to earth, and earth to primordial chaos below; beneath the city God placed the source of all waters, fount of the rivers of the Garden of Eden. So Jerusalem's water was the sweetest and purest in the world and its dew better than any medicine. There, where no man or woman ever suffered injury, Solomon's wisdom would restore her to Dod.

On occasion Shulamith had glimpsed the King passing nearby on his way to the summer palace on

Mount Lebanon. Exhaling myrrh and frankincense, his cortege rose from the South like columns of smoke. Sixty battle-skilled warriors, sword on thigh, escorted the royal palanquin with its posts of silver, top of gold, seat of purple wool, interior inlaid lovingly with ivory by his harem. Flowers were painted throughout, people said, intertwined with descriptions of the power of love. Solomon reclined inside, wearing the crown his mother Bathsheba had placed atop his brow on his wedding day to the Egyptian princess. Tawny-skinned and hollow-eyed, the King's massive head seemed to reflect his teaching that wisdom comes from the head and its mind—and not, as David had said, from the heart and its feelings. If a child's face is the gift of God and a man's face his own doing, Solomon was the self-created great lion of Judah, who held Israel's foes at bay.

Finally morning came. Shulamith arose and prepared cakes of barley and figs and a skin of sour milk, all the while praying for God to safeguard her journey, for she had dreamed the world was full of holes and she feared falling out of it.

Indeed, no sooner had the girl set out to Jerusalem than she was snatched up and whirled around till she was encircled by her own screams. Breaking

free, she tumbled to the ground, rolled over arms
and legs and—

"*Dod!*"

"Did you miss me?"

"Miss you!" She hugged him fiercely. "O Dod!
If only you were my brother. Then I could kiss you
in front of all Shunem, and people wouldn't scorn
me. I could bring you inside my home, where I'd
give you my spiced wine—"

"Is that all?" He drew her down beneath an
apricot tree.

Looking up, she saw him crowned with pale
rose-colored blossoms, their centers blushing carmine.
His left hand, rough as bark, cushioned her head
and caressed it.

"Does Ben ever do this?"

"No . . ."

"Or Asa . . . this?" His right arm, sturdy as a
tree trunk, encircled her.

She closed her eyes and shook her head.

Dod laughed. "Then why wish I were a
brother?" His lips traced the contours of her face and
throat. "You are fair, my love, so fair! Your eyes are
like doves . . . your hair black as the goats trailing
down Mount Gilead . . . teeth like newly shorn sheep

41

. . . cheeks like pomegranates . . . lips like bands of
scarlet . . . mouth so comely . . . breasts like fawns
. . . Every part of you is fair, my love, without a
blemish . . . You have ravished my heart."

She sobbed.

"Shulamith! What is it?"

She told of her forced betrothal to Mushi. Nobody, he vowed, would marry her but him. How long
would it take Dod to match her cousin's bride-price?
If he left Shunem to work in the city or the copper
refinery, or sailed with the King's merchant fleet on
its three-year voyages, perhaps six years.

"Our only hope then is Solomon."

"That green bay tree?" Dod scoffed. "He's as
indifferent to commoners as that sixty-foot evergreen
to all the stunted trees around it. If the King cared at
all about his people, he'd stop working us and taxing
us, so that your brothers and I could afford to marry.
Solomon's *horses* live better than we . . ."

Did other girls contemplate men's faces and
bodies while they spoke? Surely not virgins. Ashamed,
Shulamith nevertheless kept studying Dod as if trying to memorize him. Surely any girl who concen-
trated only on a man's words did not truly love him.

"I know! Shulamith, we'll ask Jeroboam for help.
He was my overseer, but he sympathizes with us

workers. So much so, the Northern elders want him to petition Solomon to lighten the people's yoke, though he says it's useless. Jeroboam compared the King to the Sea of Salt. It takes the good waters from the Jordan but never gives a drop away—that's what makes it stagnant." He burst out, "That Solomon! He beats us like flax. If only he knew how to live—or when to die."

"Dod!"

Yet neither of them wanted to talk about Solomon when they could enjoy silence together. With a look, a touch, caresses.

My beloved is mine and I am his, Shulamith delighted to think. Now she and Dod could run through the field, gather lilies, lodge amid the henna blossoms. There she might even tender Dod her love, which she had stored up for him only.

"So!" Ben had descended upon them too soon. "This is how you keep your own vineyard, Shulamith!"

Dod jumped to his feet. "I want to marry your sister. Let me substitute service for the *mohar*, as Jacob did for Rachel. I'll work for you and Asa seven years. Fourteen years—"

"Fine," said Ben. "That would give us more shepherds than we have sheep."

43

"Something else then. *Anything*."

"Like the bride-price Saul asked David for the Princess Michal?"

"A hundred Philistine foreskins!"

"Who wants your death in battle or a foreskin necklace?" More apologetic than angry, Ben beseeched Dod even as he tried to push him away, "Just leave now, at once, before you ruin everything for everyone."

Too late. At the head of a procession of servants bringing the *mohar*, Mushi appeared, his girth that of a glutton and his face full of broken commandments.

Shulamith wept.

"We all live not as we wish," said Ben, looking away, "but as we can."

At the same time that Asa was motioning Dod to leave, Mushi held out his hands in welcome, declaiming piously, "Our sages have instructed us to seek a wife not for money, but for modesty, respectable family, mild temper, industry, tact."

"An exact description of our little sister," Asa put in.

"Even if she weren't, Shulamith is a virgin beauty, and I like nothing better in a woman than virginity. Unless it's experience. But her experience must be mine, all mine." Mushi unslung a skin of

44

wine from his shoulder. "Shall we drink to love, my bride?" Unstopping the skin, he squeezed it with both hands and drank deeply.

Oh! Imagine those hands clutching her. Mushi was unclean.

"Here." He shoved the wineskin at Shulamith. "I like my brides bubbling."

She felt sick.

"Drink up now. This is how you do it." Mushi wrung both her breasts till she thought they would come off in his hands. "Maybe I'm marrying wrong; the wineskin's bosom is bigger than yours." He laughed. "Squeeze!"

"Like this?" With all her might she squirted the wine into her cousin's eyes.

With all his might Dod slammed Mushi against Ben and Asa, felling all three. And before any of them could jump to his feet, Shulamith and Dod had fled toward Jerusalem.

# SOLOMON

David had selected the worst possible site for a capital, Solomon thought every time he approached Jerusalem. For the city had no natural advantages: no important spring within its walls, no rich fields for grain, no easy access for other nations, no harbor, no river frontage, like Babylon on the Euphrates and Thebes on the Nile. Fertile Hebron should have remained Israel's capital, but to unite the ten Northern tribes with the South's Judah and to avoid jealousy, David had conquered a neutral Canaanite stronghold between them and moved the capital there. Cut off by deep valleys from the main caravan routes and guarded by ravines on the east, west and south, the City of David lay waterless on a limestone plateau. Only the wisdom of Solomon could have transformed thirteen acres of barrenness into one of the world's largest cities, second only to the capitals of Egypt and Assyria.

Returning now from his overnight stay in Ezion-Geber, the King watched as the fingerlike hill of the City of David rose out of the wilderness to beckon him. An opulent pink crown of dressed stone walls and tall towers, it was modeled after the heavenly Jerusalem, and Solomon rejoiced as much to come home as he had rejoiced the week before to escape. How, he puzzled, could one devoid of all energy be so restless!

The arrival of the King with his entourage interrupted the city's commerce, as thousands of swirling people paused to render him homage. Pack trains unloading tribute, officials bringing taxes, soldiers guarding the gate, beggars squatting in the dust, foreign dignitaries departing, laborers awaiting daily hire, scribes offering to write letters, administrators going to work, shoppers haggling with traders, caravans of ivory, spices, and perfumes arriving, skilled alien workers hawking their wares, merchants displaying goods, wives going from weavers to jewelers to cabinetmakers, many of them foreign . . . the

Tower of Babel reassembled. Only no confusion of tongues here, Solomon noted with pride: foreigners and Israelites alike spoke the King's language.

So pink did the walls of Jerusalem glow that afternoon, they seemed to be originating sunlight instead of reflecting it. Shining reminders of Jeroboam, for he had overseen their construction. While the Prince awaited his father's death, perhaps plotted it, the orphaned Jeroboam had been building Israel and a great name. Solomon inquired about him of a Northern governor who was delivering his district's monthly provisions for the royal court, and was told the commander was due there the following day.

"Good!" exclaimed Solomon. "A splendid man, my commander, isn't he?"

"Everyone likes Jeroboam." The governor hesitated before adding, "He's smoother than cream and his words are softer than oil."

The King proceeded into the palace compound. A high wall, guarded by Philistine mercenaries, separated the City of David from the House of the Forest of Lebanon, the treasury; the Hall of Pillars, waiting room for those petitioning the King; the Hall of Judgment, with the Throne Room; and the chief Queen's private palace, adjacent to Solomon's Palace. Overlooking all of Jerusalem on the northernmost point of the hill-city rose the House of God, its massive twin pillars nudging the heavens.

No house of prayer, for the people prayed in its courtyard and never inside, the Temple proclaimed that the Lord dwelt with the King. Its nearness prevented priests from usurping the throne, as had happened in Egypt. Similarly, Solomon's introduction of foreign gods on the Mount of Olives opposite, where he built them shrines, made it difficult for Israelite prophets to speak in the name of the One God. No sense in chancing another Samuel, who secretly anointed David as King when Saul stopped heeding the prophet.

As Solomon strode into the Palace, swirling gusts sanded him, foretastes of the sirocco that neither cooled nor cleaned. The sultry southeastern wind parched the mouth and inflamed the eyes, while the wintry northeastern desert winds numbed body and spirit. Successive siroccos and winter rains had tinged the white limestone the delicate rose-ivory of a baby's complexion. But Solomon's skin they had turned a yellowish brown. How long, he wondered, before they would do as much for his bones?

What a relief to enter his chamber. No need when alone to stride, to acknowledge acclaim, to bear himself with a majesty he no longer felt, to resist the pull of the earth. Once inside, Solomon closed his eyes and slumped against the polished bronze wall of the vestibule.

"My lord!"

The King straightened up. "Who is there?" He could not see, for the vestibule's endless reflections of torchlight—designed to blind whoever entered— had dazzled him.

"It's Isis, my lord."

Isis—wise, dignified, kind—who does a man good and never evil all her days. Yet he avoided the chief Queen as he did his own mirror. For day after day he could see time chipping at her like a vindictive sculptor, cutting away her roundness, lining her face with fretwork, chiseling its features to sharpness, shriveling and blanching the Egyptian till her wigs grew larger and blacker in contrast. Age, alas, had cuckolded him.

"Forgive my intrusion. I thought you were still in Ezion-Geber."

Stepping inside the chamber, Solomon saw Isis standing beside his bed. Her shame at being discovered there made him feel himself the intruder. Had she been reliving their wedding some thirty years before? Its celebration had surpassed even that of the completion of the Temple, for the last Israelite involved with a pharaoh's daughter had been Moses. Serenaded by a thousand Egyptian musical instruments, Solomon vowed that night to memorialize Isis' name in Israel with more sons than she had ancestors. And while he slept, his chief wife covered the windows and bed canopy with black tapestries so that, awaking and thinking it night still, he lay with her till noon.

". . . such a joy to see the sun again after the rains, to feel its warmth," she was saying. ". . . how sweet the light . . ."

"No sun shines for me," Solomon retorted. "All my days now are nights. Nights without sun, moon or star."

"A dirge on a spring day? Such ingratitude."

"Better to go to a house of mourning than to a banquet hall. That's the end of all men."

" 'Better is the end of a thing than its beginning.' "

Solomon frowned. "It's impolite to contradict me with my own proverb."

Isis allowed herself a smile. "Who else is wise as Solomon?"

Wise! "Had I been truly wise, I'd have spent my days seeking a way to fight off death. There's no discharge in that battle." He unbuckled his sword

54

and laid it on the bed. "A battle with the same out-
come for beast and man. As the one dies, so dies the
other: both have the same life-breath. Both come from
dust and both return to dust, and who knows if man's
spirit rises upward and if a beast's sinks down into
the earth?"

"If my lord will allow me." Isis touched her
collar necklace made of dozens of tiny carved plaques
of gold. "This usek was given the first pharaoh at the
sunrise of time, and each successive pharaoh passed
it down to his child, everyone adding another golden
link—"

Solomon interrupted. "And now it is yours forever. So?"

The Queen reddened as if slapped.

Why did unhappy people always seek to make
converts? "Isis—"

She averted her eyes. "I deserve your hatred. A
child is love made flesh." Softly she recited one of
Solomon's few psalms, " 'Children are a heritage of
the Lord, the fruit of the womb is a reward. As arrows
in the hand of a mighty man, so are the children of
one's youth. Happy is the man that has his quiver
full of them. He shall not be put to shame.' "

Four things are never satisfied: fire, earth, the
grave, a barren womb. How Isis, named after the

Egyptian goddess of fertility, had striven for mother-hood. Through amulets, magic, vows, mandrake roots, journeys to the Northern baths for blasts of hot air and steaming waters tinged with the blood of sacrificial sheep. And when holding Solomon's wives and concubines in her lap while they gave birth did not avail her either, the sinless Isis concluded she had sinned, and fasted till her knees tottered. Now she also implored the Lord God of Israel for children, even as the King hinted to her gods about long life.

Contritely Solomon said, "I don't hate you, Isis. You know that."

"You don't love me. That's hatred enough."

What could he say? Old love, cold love? Love makes time pass, but time makes love pass? Why must you be so spiteful as to continue loving me? "Isis, you were telling me about your usek."

"Yes, my lord." She fondled the gold collar. "Perhaps if you were to see yourself not merely a solitary man whose day will end, but like this necklace, part of the stream of life flowing from your Adam and Eve to the remote future—"

"Flowing through Rehoboam?" Such a son only a barren woman would not abhor. "He's what makes me detest my life's work. Because I must leave it all to him." The King shook his head in wonder. "David sought might; I developed my mind; my firstborn cultivates neither. Alas, children always disappoint parents."

"Could it be," suggested Isis, "because parents very often disappoint their children?"

Solomon scowled. "When I want wisdom, I'll get a scribe to read me my three thousand proverbs."

The Queen turned away. "My lord did not speak to me like that when we married. When Solomon loved me, we could have slept together on the edge of a knife. Now that he doesn't, a bed as large as Jerusalem is not wide enough for us."

True, a year after their wedding Solomon was the one masking the windows and canopy in order to keep her in bed till noon. "I wish nothing had changed, Isis." He never so much wanted to love her as when he discovered he had stopped. "With all my heart I wish that."

"I know, my lord, I know. But what comfort is knowledge?" She busied herself with the bed, turning down the coverlet and placing his sword by his pillow. "Come, lie down. You must be tired after your long journey."

"Yes. I feel the earth is dragging me down into its bowels."

Isis helped him disrobe. When he lay down, she

rubbed his back until his heart relaxed. Maybe he would ask her to stay the night, and extend it by masking the windows. He couldn't remember the last time he had made love to a woman he loved.

But then she said, "Let me get my harp and play for you."

The King stiffened. "No! Never! You think me another Saul?"

"My lord? I don't understand—"

"Go now. Leave me."

After Isis withdrew, Solomon tried to forget that when the spirit of the Lord departed from King Saul and evil spirits terrified him, he sought out a skillful player on the harp to drive them away. That was David. He later usurped the throne, and Saul went mad.

But why dwell on past misfortune when he had Jeroboam's visit to anticipate? The King closed his eyes and hoped for hope.

Inside the Throne Room, lined with more soldiers than cedar panels, court officials reverently greeted Solomon the next morning, as ready for the day's business as he was not. The King strode through

the scrapings of foreheads against floor, then mounted
the gold steps of his ivory throne, whose royal chair
overlooked six elevations, like its divine model in
seventh heaven.

"Good morning, my lord."

Zabud, the King's middle-aged chief minister
and son of Nathan the prophet, who had denounced
David's adultery with Bathsheba. Only Israel among
the nations allowed prophets to speak in the name of
God without fear of royal reprisal—something to be
proud of. Also wary. To forestall challenges to his
authority, early in his reign Solomon had subordi-
nated the priests and absorbed Zabud by appointing
him chief minister. So well had that worked, or so
poorly, that Zabud now echoed the King's words before they were uttered—a verbal form of self-abuse.

"My lord looks especially well today."

A laying on of words. Clearly the physician had
alerted Zabud that Solomon was ill.

"Shall we begin, my lord?"

One of these days my lord would say no. But
who then would develop new cities, iron resources, a
bigger navy, increased trade, a vaster army, more
alliances, additional enterprises, and constantly build
public works and highways for Israel?

"Begin."

Amid much unrolling of papyri, reports followed on an Israel that Solomon's shepherd father could never comprehend. Finances, taxes, forced labor, industries, defenses, the army and the navy, tribute from the once-dreaded Philistines and other foes, caravan tolls, public works, the twelve administrative districts . . .

Forty years of the same reports. No wonder Solomon could concentrate on them no longer and his thoughts scattered. When asked for an opinion now, he found it hard to frame a reply. Officials presented two choices, and he rejected both because he couldn't decide on one. Then a governor inquired about Solomon's plans for the future—

"What future?" Dreariness . . . numbness . . . loneliness . . . the pit. *"Enough!"*

Solomon had the room emptied. Slowly he descended the throne and shuffled to the window to gaze outside at the indifferent sky. Presently a fluttering heart and dull chest pains sent him pacing the floor. God in heaven! Would he ever feel well again?

"Good morning, Father."

Rehoboam. He had trailed Solomon back to Jerusalem, like a jackal sniffing after the blood of a wounded lion.

"A favor, my lord." The Prince worked at his smile. "Since you won't appoint me co-regent, may I at least practice being King? Under your guidance. After all, one day I will be King—"

"With the connivance of the Angel of Death."

Rehoboam pouted. "Please, Father. It's hard enough understanding you when you say exactly what you mean. My lord? May I sit in judgment this morning over your petitioners?"

This request was not unreasonable, however unreasoning Rehoboam would prove to be. "Very well."

The Prince bounded up the six gold steps as if to his anointment. He pawed the ground beneath the overhanging carved dove whose claws were set in a hawk. Though he said nothing, his heavy breathing cried out, At last! Finally!

"A little more decorum." Solomon pointed to the gold lions flanking each elevation. "Else my pets will eat you."

"Oh, Father." Seating himself, Rehoboam propped his feet on the gold footstool and rapturously fingered the royal chair's overlay of beryls, emeralds, rubies, and pearls. "I feel a thousand feet tall!"

"Feel taller than your father? I wouldn't want sitting on the throne to give you ideas."

"Father," Rehoboam assured him, "I never have ideas."

The King sighed. "That I believe." A signal brought Zabud back.

The chief minister, seeing Rehoboam enthroned, looked crestfallen, for he considered himself as much part of the King as the crown. Solomon explained that the Prince would judge that day's petitioners, and the chief minister withdrew, muttering, "How the puny have risen."

"King!" exulted Rehoboam. "It's like being God." When Solomon pointed out that no monarch lives so long, the Prince declared, "But as long as he lives, the King has the power to raise up or cast down, make or unmake, grant life or decree death. Exactly like the Lord. To judge all, but be judged by none."

Solomon shuddered. "Your first lesson, Rehoboam. You may think you're divine, but the people do not. In Israel it is not the King who is sovereign, but God's Law. Egypt's pharaoh may claim to be a god, but I'm not even the Lord's son-in-law. The Israelite way is wiser, of course: claim to be a god, and people will expect you to pass miracles."

"Nevertheless," Rehoboam argued, "the King's authority is absolute."

"Not in Israel. Here all are brothers before God. So Nathan the prophet reminded David when he cuckolded Uriah. My father's sovereignty derived from a covenant with the people under the Law, as did his obligation to rule with justice. And since the King rules by Law, he himself is subject to it. Now what is it, Rehoboam? You look confused."

"Your words I understand this time, Father. But—"

"But what?"

"Why can't I rule as *you* have always ruled?"

Two petitioners were announced before Solomon could respond. Retreating into the shadow of the throne, he was pleased that though Rehoboam welcomed the farmers as if they were the Queen of Sheba, one of them cried out in distress,

"*You* are not Solomon."

The man in the right, concluded the King.

Annoyed, Rehoboam drummed his fingers on the bejeweled armrest. "I am the *imminent* King of Israel."

The farmer turned to go. "We'll return next week."

"*Now*," shouted the Prince. "Unless you wish to be fined for wasting my royal time."

Swiftly the other farmer presented his suit.
Sometime before, the two were working in a field,
when Elchanan grew faint from lack of food. So he
borrowed a boiled egg from Abishai, vowing to repay the egg's worth.

Rehoboam chuckled. "One egg—that's a problem?"

"But had I hatched the egg, I'd have had a
chicken, which would have hatched ten more, each
capable of producing another ten since that time.
Now I demand ten times ten times ten chickens, for
a total of one thousand."

"Abishai wants to take everything I own and
sell my family and me into slavery," moaned Elchanan. "All for a single egg."

"A problem indeed," Rehoboam conceded. "Did
you swear before two witnesses to repay the egg's
worth?"

"Yes, I did, but—"

"Then I have no alternative," said the Prince,
"but to award Abishai the judgment."

As Elchanan wailed, Solomon stepped forward.
Seeing him, both farmers prostrated themselves.

"Rehoboam, you haven't set the time when Abishai should collect. May I?" The King turned to

Abishai. "Plant one boiled bean. The very moment it sprouts, Elchanan must pay you the thousand chickens."

"Yes, my lord," said Abishai. "That will take two weeks or—Did you say a boiled bean?"

"Yes, boiled. Like your egg." The King dismissed both men before Elchanan could stop crying or Abishai begin.

Agitated, Rehoboam jumped up. "You made me lose face."

"Better your face than Elchanan his family. The beginning of the Law is with benevolence, David taught, and with benevolence it ends."

"And what of the Law itself? Changing my decision will make my subjects lose respect for it."

After one sitting—*his* subjects. "True, in order to be just, the Law must be stable. I won't speak again."

The second case concerned two shepherds who accused each other of exchanging a dead lamb for a live one. This time Rehoboam knew the solution; dramatically he ordered the live lamb split between the two claimants.

Alas, neither man would yield the whole lamb instead of seeing it divided. So Rehoboam questioned them further, discovering only that the lamb could not recognize its own mother, and that one man was wealthy and the other poor.

"Well," said the Prince. "Since the beginning of the Law is with benevolence—"

Solomon, on the far side of the throne, cleared his throat.

"Yet, since God bestows wealth upon the righteous—"

The King coughed.

Rehoboam began a third time. "Then, again—"

Lest his son transgress the commandment—Do not favor the poor or show deference to the rich: judge your neighbor fairly—Solomon stepped forward. He pointed between the two men while his left hand pushed the gold lion on the throne's bottom step.

Wonder of wonders! All fourteen lions roared into life.

Both petitioners fell to the floor in terror. But only the poor one vowed never to sin again.

Furious, the Prince ordered him to forfeit five lambs to the other and ordered them both away. Then he bounded down the stairs to confront his father. "You broke your promise!"

"I never said a word."

66

"You *pointed*."

The King laughed.

"You're too strong for a monarch! Israel would be better served with a ruler who is weak."

Astonishment cut Solomon's laughter short. "How can any ruler be too strong for his country's good? Even *I* don't know the answer to that riddle, Rehoboam."

He explained: "A strong king overrides everyone, while a weak ruler opens himself to diverse views. And that makes the weaker sovereign the stronger."

Before either man could return to his place, the next petitioners were admitted. A shepherdess among the group of five ran up to the King and prostrated herself, a shapely footstool of thick black hair and gentle curves swelling with youth.

"My lord of lords!" she cried. "Yours is the greatness and the power and the glory and the victory and the majesty. You are supreme."

How the girl adored her King! Solomon should scold her for mistakenly addressing to him David's last public prayer to the Lord God. Yet how comforting that at least for this girl, the King's greatness was real. Perhaps seeing it reflected in her adoring eyes would make it real for Solomon too. "Stand."

Rising, she dazzled him with a radiance like the dawn's. Surely God had lingered over this girl's creation. "Sun, moon, and star!"

"Is it true," she asked, her black eyes round with wonder, "that creation began here? That Adam was formed from the dust of Jerusalem?"

Solomon smiled. "So people say."

"And that no woman ever miscarried in Jerusalem, no fire ever broke out in Jerusalem, no building ever collapsed in Jerusalem? That only the most beautiful women and handsomest men live in Jerusalem?"

The King shook his head. "*You* don't live here. Who are you?"

She bowed her head. "Shulamith, my lord. From Shunem."

Shunem! The village of David's Abishag, the virgin he was too old to know. "Rehoboam, *I* shall judge this case." The King should return to his throne, but it was too distant from this delectable maiden. "Shulamith," he exclaimed, "you are fair as the moon!"

Ashamed, she hid her tanned face in her hands. "I am black, I know—"

"But *exquisite!*"

She bit her lower lip. "Please don't make fun

of me because I'm swarthy. My brothers were angry; they made me labor in their vineyards in the scorching sun, thus my own vineyard I couldn't tend."

"You don't know you're beautiful? Hasn't everyone told you?"

"Dod says I'm comely," she said artlessly, "but he loves me."

A young shepherd raced forward. "I'm Dod. Shulamith is mine."

*Never!* For a moment Solomon thought he had voiced his thought, but then a fat man in white wool inserted himself between Dod and Shulamith, his age theirs combined, and echoed aloud, "Never! Her brothers have accepted my marriage offer." He grabbed her hand and kissed it.

The girl recoiled. "He defiled my fingers!"

"You'll make me forget my manners," Mushi said self-righteously. "To this day I have never struck a woman—who wasn't my wife."

Solomon asked, "Why would any man force himself on a girl so unwilling?"

"The husband of a thousand wives must know how balky virgins are until marriage breaks them. My first wife behaved like Shulamith." Mushi burst into laughter. "To keep her from running away on our wedding night, I had to hide all her clothes."

69

"Have you dared return them yet?" asked Shula-mith.

Solomon said, "You have another wife?" Then the girl, poor as she was, spurned wealth when all other people wanted what they had not. Another reason for the King to admire her. He had amassed countless treasures before appreciating their worthlessness.

Mushi preened. "I have *two* wives, my lord. And two concubines. I believe a man should always be in love. That's why I always marry. Every seven years."

"And the concubines?"

"Seven years is a long time between wives," said Mushi. "My lord is my model. I follow in your footsteps, so to speak."

Solomon scowled. "My unions are political. Where David used the sword, I employ nuptials. The peace of the world, after all, rests in my hands."

Mushi grinned. "One thousand political couplings?"

"You think I live my life in the bedchamber, do you?"

"Is there a better way? A thousand wives! God grant me the luxuries of life," he prayed. "I can live without the necessities."

"A thousand? How people love to exaggerate a few hundred women." Solomon knew that Israelites also believed the Queen of Sheba had journeyed to Jerusalem solely to bed him, when her motive was entirely commercial. She had come to draw up a trade treaty because the King's merchant fleet was affecting her caravan trade. Only afterward had they made love.

"Nothing wrong with extravagance, of course, so long as it's practiced with magnificence such as my lord's." Mushi leered. "How many wives and concubines and maids *are* in your harem?"

Solomon shrugged. "To count them would be unmannerly."

"*I'd* love to count them!" Mushi rubbed his fingers together, as if envisioning a census of nipples.

"Would you? Your wish is hereby granted. Go, tally all the nations in the world: that's the number of Daughters of Jerusalem—after multiplying by three or four, maybe ten. You may start at once."

The leer changed to a twitch. "My marriage— Solomon's judgment—"

Surrender so comely a being to Mushi? It would be akin to feeding a peacock to a wildcat. "Suppose we let Shulamith decide."

"But she despises me!"

"She does? Then you know her decision—"

"But, my lord!"

71

"—and mine." Solomon pointed to the door. "*Go.* Before I begin *subtracting* wives from you."

As Mushi dragged himself out, muttering, Shulamith and her shepherd embraced so tightly they seemed to fuse. How the King envied them! His arms had never succeeded in enclosing happiness, as theirs clearly did. Never before had he felt so shut out. Jealous of Dod with his armful of love, Solomon envied the girl even more for her innocence, spirit, joy, youth—everything he himself possessed no longer.

The older brother approached Shulamith, saying, "Know that Solomon's judgment does not displease me." But the younger one yelled at her, "Selfish!" Both wanted to take their sister home.

So did the shepherd. He insisted on a second judgment.

Rehoboam intervened. "Father, let me resolve this matter."

"You'd have the girl go with you," Solomon stated.

"How did you know!"

The younger brother ran up to Rehoboam. "How much do you offer?"

Hurrying inside, Zabud interrupted the proceedings with an announcement. "A group of Northern elders has arrived, headed by Jeroboam."

"Jeroboam!" If only he had been exchanged in his cradle with Rehoboam, mused the King. Yet who had sired the child he deserved? Adam fathered a murderer, Abraham a nonentity, Jacob nine would-be-fratricides, Moses no-accounts, Saul an heir who meekly yielded his kingdom to a shepherd. And David —had he deserved Solomon? "Admit them at once."

Rehoboam burst out, "That Jeroboam. He whores after power."

"And you, my son, lust more decorously?" The King searched for a parable, his invention to refresh people with the Law's well of profundity, whose depth could not be plumbed other than with a single bucket of words at a time. "In the beginning the moon was created as bright as the sun. Do you know how she became so pale? Because the moon spoke jealously of the sun, God diminished the moon's light and splendor forever." Solomon looked to see the girl's reaction to his words, then wondered why he did so.

When Jeroboam entered with the Northern elders, the King rushed to greet them first. How impressive this handsome thirty-year-old stalwart, tall and straight as a spear, with a mane of walnut-brown hair rivaling Absalom's. A pity Jeroboam's father never lived to see his commanding son, advancing now on the throne with regal self-assurance.

The commander bowed low. "My lord." So polite a response? Without even asking after Solomon's health, as was customary, he began brusquely. "This is why we have come. To demand—"

The Prince interrupted. "Father, you promised to let me judge."

"No small honor," Jeroboam remarked, "to be judged by the Prince of petulance."

While Rehoboam sputtered, Solomon motioned him to the royal chair. A talk between Prince and commander should truly test his son's ability to rule. And amuse.

This time Rehoboam inched his way up the throne's steps, as if in imitation of the moon rising. Reclining beneath the dove and hawk, he waved a hand. "Begin."

Jeroboam's right arm shot out like an arrow. "Your father has made our yoke insufferably heavy. We ask his oppression be lifted. Then the North will serve faithfully."

Solomon's ears throbbed. Had he heard aright?

74

Gasps from the Shunemites affirmed he had. Swiftly the King glanced at the girl. What must she think of him now?

". . . David, shepherd of his people, shared our burdens. Solomon eats up the people as he eats bread . . ."

Again David! *Always* David. How unfair! The mason's trowel can never rival the sword and the harp.

". . . forced four months each year to quarry stones and hew timber and work the King's lands. Thirteen years alone spent on building this palace compound, when seven years sufficed for the Temple. And taxes to support Jerusalem and the rest of Judah fall on the ten Northern tribes, who foolishly traded their independence for one man's rule . . . Solomon's policies have forced shepherds and small farmers off the land into the cities in search of jobs, while enriching government officials, landowners, merchants. All hail the King's two latest inventions: the rich and the poor!"

A tongue like a sword, words like poisoned knives. How to explain that to fashion a free state, forced labor was essential; and to ensure a people's financial future, they had to be taxed? Just as liberty survives only when it is limited, and in order to preserve the equality of all, one person must rule. And could forty years of peace have been maintained without a mighty unified army? "Government, you must understand, is paradox. *Life* is paradox—"

"Father, let me." Rehoboam jumped up and addressed the commander with cold glee. "Petition denied! And if you think my father has made your yoke heavy, I'll make it heavier when *I* become King. If my father has chastised you with whips, I'll lash you with thorns. Because my little finger is thicker than Solomon's loins."

Jeroboam retorted, "Briefly spoken, my Prince." To the King: "By your leave." He motioned the elders to follow him out.

"One moment!" cried Solomon.

The commander paused. "My lord?"

"You are young, so you would not know. You could not know, else you would appreciate. When I ascended the throne, Jerusalem was thirteen acres of paupers and crooked ugliness. A tent housed the Holy Ark, the Altar was unhewn stone. I raised this people like babes, built them cities, roads, fortifications, widened their cultural boundaries. I enriched everyday life with commerce, industry, arts; opened Israel to the world and the world to Israel. That's why today this land lights the four corners of the earth."

A Northern elder spoke up. "But at what cost, my lord? Bent backs and people sucked dry."

"Greatness, power, glory, victory, majesty— these cannot be bought cheaply."

"Isn't that why Solomon had to sell twenty cities of Galilee to the King of Tyre?" asked another elder. "Wasting Israel's substance on erecting buildings without souls while people go hungry. My lord, nobody can eat stones."

Ingratitude encompassed him like bees! True, Solomon had never learned thrift, but he had made a poor, small nation rich and great. And why shouldn't peace inspire a people to sacrifice the way war does? "Isn't it better to conscript people and taxes for public works and industries than, as my father did, for cutting neighbors' throats?" Wrong, wrong, wrong. Jeroboam was the adversary here, not David. "You speak for farmers, you say. Ever grow olive trees, Jeroboam? Before engrafting, the young plant must be cultivated eight years, and afterward there's a three-year wait for fruit. But it takes over twenty years to reach its peak, after countless waterings in the beginning and half a dozen diggings each year. Yet all this effort rewards the planter and his heirs with the mature olive tree that may live forever."

The commander regarded Solomon coolly. "An

apt parable. Olives yield their oil only when crushed, and the best oil comes after the worst beatings. My lord, nobody doubts that Jerusalem shall endure forever. As Solomon's pyramid, entombing a live people with a—" He broke off.

A dead King: Solomon's nightmare. Cold sweat drenched him. "We shall continue . . . another time . . . tomorrow . . . perhaps." His soul bowed down, he started for the door.

A smile flickered across Jeroboam's face. Why so triumphant a look? He had not won a single concession.

The shepherdess intercepted Solomon.

Such a beauty—warm, young, loving. So awed by him, as nobody else was any longer. "Are you still here?"

She nodded. Wise girl, she knew also how not to talk.

"I'm glad." The King recalled a psalm of David: "My soul thirsts for You, my flesh longs for You in a dry and weary land without water. So have I searched for You . . ." Only, it was not the God of lovingkindness that Solomon had in mind now, but this artless girl.

The shepherd ran up and grasped Shulamith's hand. "We seek my lord's blessings on our marriage."

Another squabble. One brother wished to pull her home, the other to shove her into Rehoboam's harem; the Prince scampered down the throne to press his own claim. All contended for a simple shepherdess—and Solomon understood why. With a young girl like this beside him, any man might begin life all over again.

"Silence! We'll settle this at once." The King pointed to Dod. "You're a shepherd, aren't you? A shepherd without any sheep."

The youth nodded.

"The sages have ruled a husband owes his wife three obligations: to support her, to clothe her, and to fulfill his marital duties."

"I can do that!"

"Do what?"

The shepherd flushed. "Fulfill my marital duties."

"So can an ass. Would you have Shulamith marry an ass?"

"We love each other."

"Love does much," Solomon observed, "but money does more." Now if only he knew what did most.

Shulamith sobbed. Her older brother took her hand.

79

But the King could not entrust the girl to her brothers. They might trade her to another Mushi. So he ruled, "Shulamith remains."

The shepherd intervened between Solomon and the girl. "For what reason?"

Solomon bridled. "I have dispensed entirely too many reasons today." He signaled the guards.

"Thank you, Father," said Rehoboam. "She'll be the fairest of my concubines." He held out his arms to the girl.

Shulamith shrank from him. A girl of judgment as well.

Without first consulting her brothers, Solomon said, "Bring the girl to *my* harem."

Nobody moved, not even the guards. Everyone was struck dumb. The lawless order of the King startled them all. Himself too. How elating, his renewed decisiveness!

"*Do as I say,*" he now commanded. "*I am still King here!*"

Shulamith cried out when the guards took hold of her, and the shepherd grappled with them. Bemused, the brothers turned to Solomon. His assurance of proper compensation appeased the younger brother. But the older one reached out to her, beseeching her approval of this transaction.

She turned her head. "Dod . . ."

Jeroboam marched up to enter a protest. "My lord, you cannot—"

"On the contrary. I can, and always will be able." Solomon strode out the door.

For the first time that day, for the first time in months, he noticed sunshine pouring into the vestibule, gold liquefied, and he thought, It *is* spring . . . how sweet the light, how good to behold the sun. So long as a man lives, let him rejoice, for the days of darkness will be many, and what follows thereafter is . . . nothingness.

Somebody clutched him. Who dared! Rehoboam, so distraught he had to be forgiven, poor Prince.

"Father, you astonish me! Lusting after a sheepgirl—"

Solomon shook himself free and eyed his son disdainfully. "Only the weak can control their passions," he asserted. "They have such weak passions."

And he departed the Hall of Judgment.

# SHULAMITH

Struggling, the girl was escorted out of the Hall of Judgment. That morning she had given thanks to the Lord for bringing her safely to Jerusalem, now she regretted fleeing Shunem. What did Solomon want with her? His harem comprised enough women to overrun Egypt. What difference could one more make to the King?

She entered the harem, still struggling. Though it was sheathed in warm red cedar from floor to ceiling and ornamented by pilasters of sweet-smelling sandalwood, with freshly cut flowers spilling out of tripods and golden lamps spreading sunlight indoors, to Shulamith it was a prison.

"Daughters of Jerusalem," a guard announced, "you have a new sister."

The queens, concubines, and maids hardly looked around. "What we need," said one, "is brothers."

A garishly colored woman, enlarging her wanton eyes with black paint before a mirror, paused to remark, "Solomon is too downcast these days to indulge in women."

A guard grinned. "Surely this girl will raise him higher than his spirits. She's done as much for me, Rainbow, and I've only held her arm."

Shulamith tore herself away from him and ran to the door. Guards in bronze helmets and leather tunics turned her back. She raced to the curtained windows. Latticed. God save her!

The Daughters of Jerusalem circled Shulamith and scrutinized her as if *she* were the alien there. From the four corners of the earth they had come, from everywhere except Israel, which pleased the people as much as it displeased them. (Solomon can marry any princess in the world! Why aren't our own daughters good enough for him?) Never before had Shulamith realized that woman came in such variety, nor that there was no part of her body that jewelry could not cover, encircle, bedeck, or pierce. Most of them had the enviable yellowish-white complexion of wheat after threshing and winnowing, and bunched together in tunics of every hue, they looked like a garden in full bloom and smelled like after rain.

"What do you think, Rainbow? Will Solomon make her a concubine?"

The garish one sneered. "Easier for the sheepgirl to become a porcupine. She's an Israelite."

Somebody stepped on Shulamith's foot. "Doesn't it hurt to go barefoot?"

"If it doesn't hurt the sheep, why should it hurt her?"

Another touched Shulamith's black mantle. "Is this what Israelites wear? What do you call it?"

"Dirt."

"No, not dirt. It's her skin."

Shulamith fought back tears.

"Perhaps she's the Queen of Sheba."

"Stop!" cried the girl. "Let me be. I didn't ask to be brought here."

"You can't deceive us," said Rainbow. "Feigning reluctance to arouse the King's interest—"

"Why didn't *you* ever try that, Rainbow?" someone asked. "Think of all the paint you could save."

"No pretense," said Shulamith. "I want to escape."

"Escape?" Black-lined eyes widened, carmined lips dropped.

"Will you help me?"

"Why, guards are posted more to prevent girls from stealing into the harem than out."

"I must escape. Dod's waiting for me."

"Which prince is he?"

"Prince? Dod is a shepherd—from Shunem."

Laughter pealed. Endlessly, for the women took turns repeating Shulamith's hope to trade the Palace for a sheepfold, until she covered her ears with her hands.

*"Silence!"*

An older woman, with a huge wig of black hair and sheep's wool, appeared. Her flesh was so lean she looked like a butterfly that was turning back into a worm. The gold fillet of cobras around her head and the women's respectful attitude toward her proclaimed her the Egyptian-born chief Queen.

"The girl may be a shepherdess," said the pharaoh's daughter, "but you are the sheep." She approached Shulamith, gazed at her thoughtfully. "Now I understand why Solomon detained you. You have the face of a benediction."

"How nice," Rainbow commented. "Isis is finally with child."

Tears started in the Queen's eyes. Her hand flew to a gold collar necklace.

Shulamith touched Isis' hand. "Some people are so perfect," she said, "God despairs of repeating them in children. It was that way with my father's sister."

"You *are* beautiful." Isis cradled the girl's face in her hands. "I hope you stay with Solomon forever."

Shulamith pulled away, amazed. "You say that—you, his chief wife?"

"That's why."

"But there's Dod. I love him."

"There's Solomon, whom nobody loves."

"*Everyone* loves the King."

Isis shook her head. "Everyone *wants* Solomon for something. The Daughters of Jerusalem want more quarters, more luxury, more time; they want more of everything. And less is what the people wish: less taxes, less conscription, less rule. Jeroboam seeks the King's life. Solomon's own son prays for his death."

Shulamith gasped.

"The King has nobody—nobody who wants nothing of him but to serve."

"He has you."

The Queen sighed. "I am no different. I too want something: my love requited. How easy to be a man. All he has to do is exercise his passions. But a woman must provoke them—continually. How terrible to be shut up till death in widowhood, while one's husband still lives."

Shulamith recalled that when Michal scorned David for dancing half naked before the Holy Ark, he left her to die childless. That demonstrated David's love of God, some said. But Shulamith always thought it God's opposite, hard-heartedness.

Ripples of excitement. "A man!" someone shouted. "No, Rehoboam."

Ignoring the Daughters of Jerusalem, the Prince darted to Shulamith. "I must speak to you," he said. "Alone."

The Queen embraced the girl. "Consider what I have said. For you it means a few brief days. But they are Solomon's forever." And she left.

Shulamith started after Isis, but Rehoboam stopped the girl. "Shepherdess, I have wonderful news. Wait till you hear!" He shook her arm. "You're not listening. Don't you remember who I am?"

"Of course." Mushi's royal counterpart, as small and thin as her cousin was mountainously fat, and equally loathsome. "Solomon's son."

"I am Rehoboam the Prince. A father in my own

right. I have half a dozen children or so, with more to come."

Shulamith, who would have died for her father, studied Rehoboam. "Can it be true what the Queen said—?"

"Who cares what Isis said? She's old. But I didn't seek you out to talk about her—"

"Nor me, I'm sure. Something regarding yourself?"

"Of course. And you too." He grasped her hand and fumbled with it. "Shulamith, you are a comely shepherdess, and when they wash you off and dress you up, perhaps comelier. I must have you. Come join *my* harem. There you'll at least be a concubine."

She suppressed a smile. Shunemites spoke with more ardor to goats than Rehoboam addressed girls, for all his thick loins.

He took her silence for bargaining. "Not a concubine then. Be my wife, if you insist. Yes, I will marry you, even though you are what you are."

*"Wife?"*

"Yes, that is generous of me, isn't it?" He pointed to the ceiling. "I'll place your throne higher than those of all my other queens. You will wear the royal crown." Fervently he added, "And so will *I*."

"Solomon—"

The Prince snorted. "Oh, my father will never make you a queen. Who are you? Nobody's daughter. What profit in allying himself with the sheep of Shunem. Wool he despises as does the Egyptian royalty, who won't wear it even when they die. No, Solomon would keep you here only until you'd tire him; and from what I hear, that would be overnight. And then, back to the goats with you. Shulamith, you must tell my father."

"Tell him what?"

"That you wish to be my queen, of course."

Why did she provoke the worst of men to matrimony? "But I don't."

"That's foolish. Of course you do. What Israelite girl would refuse the imminent King? Marrying me makes you nearly divine. One thing, however: you must tell Solomon this idea is yours."

"I don't understand—"

"Good."

Rehoboam left Shulamith bewildered. From Shunemite shepherdess to Queen of Israel in one hour!

Servants brought her foods she could not recognize: not a barley cake or sycamore fig among them. As soon as she finished eating, the Daughters of Jerusalem carried her off and stripped her. Trying to hide behind her hands, she was pulled and shoved till the floor melted beneath her into a pool of water. And when she surfaced, they tried to drown her.

"Stop fighting us! Haven't you ever had a bath before?"

Afterward they rubbed her with soft white wool till her skin tingled. She felt curiously mothered.

"What vision Solomon has. Underneath, the sheepgirl *is* comely."

They anointed her body with sweet-smelling myrrh and oiled her hair and combed it, weaving pearls throughout, like drops of white dew. Then they dressed her in a tunic of fine blue linen embroidered with gold flower rosettes, and leather sandals encrusted with beads, and bedecked her with jewelry until she could not move without jangling.

"Now you look like an *elegant* sheepgirl," said Rainbow. "Maybe Solomon will be able to kiss you without holding his nose."

When Shulamith looked into a mirror, she hardly knew herself. The Daughters of Jerusalem had adorned her cheeks with plaited wreaths and hung all kinds of precious stones around her neck.

93

Rainbow led the girl through quarters larger than Galilee to a private chamber. "I hope Solomon is not *too* disappointed," she remarked before she left.

A divan with purple cushions on an elevated frame dominated the room and announced its purpose. Had Shulamith fled Mushi and withstood the Prince only to end with another who was not Dod? She hurried to the curtained windows. More lattices.

Footsteps echoed down the corridor outside. Where to hide? The curtains. She slipped behind them as the King entered with his chief minister.

". . . plucking a girl from her family, like a grape off the vine. I have never known my lord to act so recklessly."

"Reason was against it, I know. That's why I thank God for my impulses."

"But it's unseemly for the great Solomon to conscript a shepherdess."

"Was it? Then I am unseemly."

"It's not *politic.* You'd have been wiser to seize Jeroboam."

"He may not concur with my policies. Nevertheless, Jeroboam is a man of superb ability."

"And ambition—don't omit that. Ambition that sneaks rather than soars. That man means to overthrow you—"

94

"Zabud! I'd rather be betrayed by Jeroboam than distrust him. What happened earlier—I can't understand myself responding with argument instead of reason. Unless—Zabud, how much truth did Jeroboam speak?"

"Facts, some; truth, none. The *fact* is people today are unhappy; the *truth* is we have advanced from the simple farmers' life with its naïve faith. The *truth* is Solomon has led Israel from primitiveness to commerce and industry; the *fact* is not everyone can maintain your pace. Yet is that any reason to fall back? There are always people wanting their fathers to have made all the sacrifices for them, expecting material returns from the state to match their contributions. But who then will plant for those to come after us? My lord, *this* is the truth: only the blind look at a work of art and see its cost. But who can set a price on Israel's future?"

Solomon heaved a great sigh. "Facts, truth, truth, facts. Zabud, I only pray you're *right*. Because one thought frightens me: what if I have been wrong? So many people I'd have misled!"

The chief minister cleared his throat. "Again, about the Shunemite," he said. "My lord, you must release her."

"*Must?* The only thing I must do, Zabud, is die."

A long silence.

When Shulamith peered out from the curtains, she saw Solomon alone. He was smoothing his black hair, pinching his cheeks pink, chewing his lips red. Strange gestures for a king. Now he threw back his shoulders and clapped his hands.

Rainbow appeared. Surprised to see Solomon by himself, her eyes flitted around the room till they lit on the curtains. But she did not give Shulamith away. "I wish to thank my lord," she said, "for my new slave, the sheepgirl."

"You mean Shulamith?"

"It has a name?"

The King smiled. "And a shepherd too. Solomon."

"That would be *bestiality*."

He laughed. "I'll chance it. Bring her here."

Instead Rainbow undulated in so many directions at once, it was a wonder her body did not fly apart. "Why bother with a sheepgirl, when you can see me dance the Machanayim?" In her flowing garment of near-transparent muslin, she shook every part of her that was movable. So fluid were her movements she seemed boneless as a snake. Head, torso, limbs twisted and thrashed too quickly for the eye to follow. Finally Rainbow coiled herself around Solomon's feet and kissed his instep.

"Very nice," he said. "*Now* will you bring me the girl?"

Her enraged expression made Shulamith laugh aloud; Rainbow was jealous. But vanity, alas, had revealed Shulamith's hiding place.

Solomon dismissed Rainbow, then pulled back the curtains. For a long time he said nothing. The way he scrutinized her! As if searching her inmost parts, fingering her soul.

"Turn around. Let me look at you."

"What can my lord see in a sheepgirl?"

"I have here sixty queens and eighty concubines but—but"—the King stumbled over his words like a boy—"but none like you. So beautiful, so sure of what will make you happy, so full of future, while I—" One hand stroked her hair. "These pearls were only strings of beads—till you put them on." The other brushed her throat. "I'll make you gold necklaces studded with silver. Would you like that?"

"Oh, yes! I could give them to my brothers in place of the *mohar*, then marry Dod. I am his, you remember."

"We are all the Lord's, Shulamith. It's God who arranges matches between men and women."

"The Lord took a poor shepherd's only ewe and gave her to the owner of tens of thousands of flocks?"

Recognizing Nathan's denunciation of David for stealing Bathsheba, Solomon rubbed his jaw. "Well done, Shulamith. Your nails are sharp and your scratches sting."

"You did abduct me. As Mushi tried to do legally."

"Are you likening Solomon to Mushi?"

"Oh, no! Never—"

"Then how can you compare our actions?"

That confused her.

He moved closer.

"My lord, you have wives!"

"So?"

"How can you be unfaithful to them? The Seventh Commandment specifies: 'You shall not commit adultery.' "

The King chuckled. *"You* are not married."

"I will be—some day—to Dod. That means knowing another man now is sinful, almost—"

"How old are you?"

"Seventeen."

Solomon threw up his hands. "You win all arguments." He pointed to the table, laden with food and wine. "Would you like to eat before or after?"

"Before or after what?" Oh! "During," she said.

"Don't be afraid of me, Shulamith," he said, then reached for her.

Sidestepping, she cried aloud, "My lord! Shall not the judge of all Israel exercise justice?"

"Haven't you heard, Shulamith? Justice is deaf." As she retreated, he pursued her, saying, "In this life the race is not to the swift, nor the battle to the brave, nor reward to the learned. Time and chance overtake them all."

"The just are in the hands of God," she insisted to the two of them, praying it were so.

That gave him pause. "But one fate befalls the just *and* the unjust. A single fate awaits all: the righteous and the wicked, the good and the impure. This is what drives men to evil while they live: they know that afterward they are off to the dead."

Shulamith pressed her attack. "God rewards good people in the end. But sinners will be punished."

"What of all the good people who suffer while evildoers prosper? That's why I commend pleasure. Nothing is better than to eat and drink and enjoy." He seized her. "Come now, Shulamith, let's rejoice while I still can." As she struggled, he pulled her

close. "As the Lord lives! I'm jealous of you, Shulamith."

Jealous? Of *her*?

"I'm so close to the grave, and you're so fresh
from the womb. Shulamith, there's eternity in you."

She thought of her father's last days, when he
spoke of her wedding he would never celebrate and
his grandchildren he would never see. "I would help
my lord. If I only knew how—"

Solomon's hands fell to his sides. "I believe you
would, Shulamith. I hoped you could. God knows I
haven't been able to help myself." He turned away
and spoke quietly. "As King over Israel, I've applied
my mind to explore all that happens beneath the
heavens, this sorry business of life which God has
inflicted upon mankind. Everything that's done under
the sun I have examined—and all of it is nothing but
vanity and chasing after wind, a crookedness not to be
straightened, a void not to be filled . . . Here I surpassed in wisdom and treasure all who ruled before
me over Jerusalem. But I soon learned that the more
wisdom the more grief, and whoever increases his
knowledge increases his pain. So I gave myself to
merriment and tasted all pleasures." A shrug. "That,
too, I found, was vanity. Revelry is senseless, and
mirth—what does it accomplish?"

He took her hand. This time she did not resist as he led her to the window and parted the curtains.

"I undertook great works." He pointed outside, but she could not tear her eyes away from him to look. "I built me mansions, planted gardens and parks with every kind of flower and fruit tree. I constructed pools of water, enough to irrigate a forest. I bought slaves, acquired stewards, amassed silver and gold and the treasures of kings. I got me male and female singers and a goodly number of concubines, all the delights of men. So I grew great, multiplying my possessions beyond those of David and Saul combined, while I still retained my wisdom. Whatever my eyes desired, I did not deny them; I deprived myself of no joy . . ."

Shulamith wondered, Is joy in things?

He slapped his hands together. "But that was all I got out of my wealth: enjoyment. When I considered my treasures, and how hard I had labored to acquire them—everything was vanity and chasing after wind . . ."

Silence.

"They say," Shulamith began hesitantly, " 'Wisdom excels folly as light excels the dark. The wise man has his eyes in his head, while the fool walks in darkness.' "

Solomon turned on her. "But I know the same fate overtakes them both. The fate of the fool will befall even me. What good, then, all my wisdom? Vanity! The wise man is no more remembered than the fool: the past is always forgotten." His hands became fists and beat the air. "Yet how *can* the wise man die like the fool! Therefore I hate life. It's all meaningless, a vanity of vanities."

Shulamith's eyes welled with tears. "I don't know what to say."

"You're wise," said Solomon wryly. "If only all people with nothing to say would say it."

She bowed her head.

"Shulamith—" He took her face between his hands. "What's this? Even from you I exact tribute, Shulamith. A tribute of tears."

She forced a smile. "Not tears. Tribute."

Abruptly he pulled away. "I talk too much, don't I? And words only multiply the futility." He strode to the door.

"My lord?"

He paused. "The patient, I see, has infected his physician. Forgive me." And he left.

*She was searching for her love. She sought Dod,*

*but could not find him. Arising, she roamed Jerusalem*
*. . . through the marketplaces . . . in the squares. She*
*sought Dod, but could not find him.*

*The watchmen of the city, making their rounds,*
*happened on her.*

*"Have you seen my love?" she asked, without*
*awaiting an answer.*

*Scarcely had she passed them, when she dis-*
*covered Dod. She held him fast, would not let him*
*go till she had brought him home, into the room*
*where she herself had been conceived.*

*"I beg you, O Daughters of Jerusalem! Don't*
*interrupt our lovemaking until—"*

A whisper in her ear. ". . . not a sound."

Shulamith let out a scream. The hand over her
mouth strangled it. But the hand felt familiar. "Dod!"
She hugged him. "How—?"

"Jeroboam bribed the guards. He concerns himself with even one Israelite, you, while the King concerns himself with one only, himself. That Solomon!
Did he—?"

She assured him nothing had happened.

"See how a great leader acts? Jeroboam said
that petitioning the King was useless, but he followed
our wishes. Now we shall do whatever Jeroboam
commands." He helped her up.

"Maybe I don't want to leave." She pointed to the room's rich adornments. "Look what you're rescuing me from."

Dod surveyed the moonlit chamber with a jealous eye. "The beams of *our* palace are cedar trees, and our rafters cypresses." He touched the boxwood divan. "Our couch is a bed of green." The pearls caught his attention. "Don't those things weigh you down?"

"Not half as much as they uplift me."

"Oh?"

She relented. "I'm teasing." She disentangled the pearls from her hair and tossed them aside. "They're only strings of beads. I'm still a plain rose of Sharon, an ordinary lily of the valley."

"Plain? Ordinary?" He kissed her. "Compared to other girls, you're a lily among thorns." Their tongues met in a caress.

Compared to other men, Dod was an apple tree in a forest. Oh! His fruit was so sweet to taste, she was growing damp with love.

". . . the wall behind the harem," he was saying. "Jeroboam is on the other side with a rope. And if anything goes wrong, the wall opposite Isis' palace."

Suddenly—voices!

Shulamith pulled Dod behind the curtains and

prayed. Everyone knew how harem trespassers were
punished. She dared not breathe. One hand she
clamped over her mouth, the other gripped Dod, as
guards entered with torchlight.

"Gone!"

"Where will they scale the wall?"

"Behind the harem."

The room dimmed.

How did the guards learn of Jeroboam's plan?
Dod did not know. Nor could he say how they would
now get past the harem guards who had betrayed
them. Clothing himself with cursing as with a garment, he reviled the King with a passion that frightened Shulamith at first, then made her jealous.

She interrupted him. "Dod, sometimes I feel you
hate Solomon more than you love me."

"Shulamith! Sometimes, out of love for others,
one *must* hate. Sometimes, out of compassion, one
must even kill."

"I'd believe that," she said, "if you looked unhappy saying so."

The curtains parted. Rainbow stood there, expos-
ing them. She was alone—she had brought no guards
with her.

"Come," she said.

They hesitated.

"You want to escape, don't you?"

She led them into the corridor. Daughters of Jerusalem lined it now, watching Shulamith and Dod with the same relief on their faces the Egyptians felt when the plagues departed the land of the pharaohs. How strange, Shulamith thought, for Israelites to be escaping the King of Israel.

In a storage room at the end of the hall, Rainbow detached broken latticework from a window. When they expressed thanks, her face hardened. "Don't be fools," she said. "In my native land I was the only princess, my father's favorite, so the perfect mortar for allying two nations. Here I became one in a thousand—and after your arrival, not even that. Not with all my foolish paints to attract Solomon—so many colors, they are noticed and I ignored, my real name forgotten. Well, among queens and princesses, a shepherdess may stand out. But outside, in a nation of shepherdesses, the King will never find you." She pushed them. "Begone."

The two climbed through the window and dropped to the ground. Guards passed nearby through the middle court. After waiting for clouds to cover the moon, they fled north. Ahead was a stairway. They ran up the steps two at a time. What could be higher than Solomon's Palace? When they reached the top at last, Shulamith had no breath left for exclaiming, *"The Temple."*

Highest spot under the sun, holiest place on earth, to which every prayer was directed . . . the navel of the world. For Israel was located in the exact center of the world, Jerusalem in the center of Israel, the Temple in the center of Jerusalem, and in the Temple's exact center the Holy of Holies, the place of God's abode on earth. There the world itself had been created.

Even Dod was awed. "Adam and Noah sacrificed here. And a thousand years ago Abraham bound Isaac here for sacrifice too." As footsteps sounded up the stairs, he added, "May Solomon be blessed with Abraham's success."

Where to hide in the open court of assembly? Even to save their lives they could not defile the Temple by entering it. People were admitted to its portico, but only priests could enter the sanctuary itself, with access to the Holy of Holies beyond limited to the chief priest on the Day of Atonement alone.

To the right, rooted in the earth's bosom, loomed the great Brazen Altar for burnt offerings—but a fire illuminated its uppermost tier, the mountain of God.

On the left, atop a dozen metal oxen facing the four corners of the earth, rested the enormous lotus-shaped cauldron used for priestly ablutions.

"The Molten Sea," said Dod, and together they ran to it. He pushed Shulamith on the back of an ox, then jumped up to help her over the laver's rim. As they slid into the waters from beneath the earth, the primeval chaos out of which God had created the heavens and the earth, guards charged into the court below.

Peering over the cauldron's lip, she watched them encircle the two free-standing bronze pillars that flanked the entrance to the Temple. Reminders of the pillar of cloud by day and of fire by night, which led the Israelites forty years through the wilderness to the Land of Promise, these giant fire altars for sacred incense upheld the earth itself.

"Frightened, Shulamith?"

In so holy a place, where the stones had set themselves without human aid and whose workers never fell ill during the seven years of its construction? Surely no harm could befall anyone in the Temple, which contained no iron of any kind, not even nails, for iron's use in weapons rendered it unfit for this symbol of peace. Still, she could not stop herself from praying.

"What frightens *me*," said Dod, "is what you said before. There are times I can't tell the difference between love and hatred. Both excite me so much, make me feel stronger, valuable. Nobody ever confesses that hating is enjoyable, but it is. How I hate myself for hating! And love you for loving."

As soon as the guards disappeared, he helped her out of the Molten Sea and to the ground. "Now to Isis' palace."

Shulamith looked up at the Temple, paused to give thanks to the Lord for keeping Dod and her alive, sustaining them and enabling them to reach holiness.

"Hurry!"

Trailing puddles from the primeval waters, they fled, Adam and Eve escaping the Garden of Eden and the Holy of Holies' cherubim instead of being chased out. But did the fiery ever-turning sword now lie ahead?

"The meeting place," she said. "Maybe the guards know about the second one also."

"Impossible. I'm the only one Jeroboam told."

Night shadows were fleeing and day breaking when they reached the Queen's palace. Jubilantly Dod pointed to the wall opposite. "See? The rope."

Shulamith hugged him. Surviving every attempt

to keep them apart meant that the Lord wanted them joined forever. He who had saved them from all dangers would now also arrange their marriage.

"We've been waiting an hour," a voice said. "What kept you two so long?" asked another.

But the voices, though belonging to two Israelite commoners, came from *inside* the wall. A moment later the royal guard surrounded the pair and carried Dod away.

Shulamith they returned to the harem, too frightened to weep. There a visitor awaited her, enraged.

"Alas!" cried Solomon. "You're like all other women—a trap more bitter than death."

Prostrating herself, she begged for Dod's release. He had come only to claim what was his. Surely the King had compassion enough not to appropriate Dod's sole possession—

"Again Dod, always Dod! A King you withstand —to give yourself to a shepherd."

"I love him."

"Why? Because he's young? As if youth itself were an accomplishment. What a wondrous achievement, being born late!" He advanced on her. "It's my own fault: coaxing you, when I should have commanded. Well, no longer." He dragged Shulamith to the divan and tore at her tunic.

"O God! Save me!" She burst into tears.

Terror-stricken, she fought him off. He grabbed her arms and pinned them to the divan. When she tried to break away, her flailing legs knocked over the table with its decanter of wine. Spilling, it stained the divan blood-red.

Abruptly, Solomon let her go. "O Lord, save *me* . . ." He arose, horrified. "I can rule everyone but myself."

"OGodGodGodGodGodGodGodGod . . ."

"That's right, Shulamith. Remember the Lord our God." He walked to the door and leaned his head against it. "Remember your Creator in the days of your youth . . . before the evil days of age befall you, when pleasure is no more. Before the sun and light and moon and stars grow dim, and clouds descend. When the hands tremble, and the legs bend, and the teeth grow few, and the eyes dim, and the ears shut, and the appetite dulls. When one starts at the voice of a bird, before all strains of music die away. When one fears heights, and terrors lurk in a simple walk. The hair grows white, like a white almond blossom, and even sex becomes a burden. Then desire fails . . .

"Finally the silver cord snaps, the golden lamp shatters, and man falls crushed into the pit. The dust reverts to the earth, and the spirit returns to God, who bestowed it . . . So man goes to his eternal home . . . *Vanity!*"

He left her, still sobbing. Only now Shulamith wept also for the King.

# SOLOMON

*...Jacob wrestling with the angel . . . No, Solomon wrestling a demon, whose wings reach from the heavens all the way to the earth. He seizes Solomon's magic ring, then flings him far away.*

*A beggar now, Solomon wanders distant lands, declaring he is the King of Israel. Lunatic, people call him, for everyone knows Solomon still reigns in Jerusalem.*

*On occasion he meets acquaintances who recognize him, and that is worse. They remind the ragged beggar of the magnificence of the court he rules no* more. Many nights he falls asleep, sated not with food but with tears.

For three years Solomon begs from land to land to atone for multiplying horses and wives and silver and gold. In one city he hires himself out as a cook in the royal household, where he falls in love with the princess. Her father banishes him to a barren desert. Starving, Solomon buys a fish. Its belly yields his magic ring, thrown into the Great Sea by the demon.

Wishing himself back to Jerusalem, Solomon finds that the demon has assumed the King's face and form all these years and ruled as him. Immediately Solomon summons the demon to judgment. To prove who he is, Solomon recites the psalm he had written upon ascending the throne:

"Grant the King Your discernment, O God, that he may judge Your people with righteousness and the poor with justice. May he save the children of the needy and crush their oppressors. May he come down like rain upon the mown grass, as showers that water the earth . . . Yes, the King will have pity on the poor, and the souls of the needy will he save."

These words further confuse the judges, who are unable to decide who is the real Solomon. For decades now, not merely three years, Solomon has been acting not at all like the King who had requested of the

*Lord solely an understanding heart, but like an im-poster . . .*

"My lord . . .?"

Fortunately, Zabud had rescued him from another nightmare.

"You called."

"In my sleep?" To spare himself Zabud's praises of the wisdom of Solomon, who needed no advice from anyone, least of all from the chief minister, but should his opinion be asked . . . the King said, "I know I am the wisest man in all the world, Zabud. Now tell me how I've erred."

His chief minister did not hesitate. "Your seizure of Shulamith's lover. It has aroused the people. They see here a repetition of the David–Bathsheba–Uriah affair."

"At last I've become the equal of David," said Solomon wryly. "In sin."

"Rumor says you've killed the shepherd—"

Solomon flared, "I don't spill blood, everyone knows that. That's why the Lord wanted me to build the Temple, not David. Red was his color, mine is gold."

"Even so, imprisoning Dod violates the King's covenant with the people."

"I was a man before I became King!" And after being King, what would he be?

Quietly Zabud responded, "If you now profane the Law, what are you?"

Yet Solomon had never entered into a covenant with the people. The tribal elders had elected his father, but not him. Appointed by David, Solomon had never exchanged vows with them. A mistake? Perhaps a covenant would have made the people his and him theirs. "Very well, Zabud. Release the shepherd tomorrow—after he's had his fright."

The chief minister did not stir.

"Now what?"

"Shulamith, my lord. Israel knows Bathsheba was at least willing. And once the people begin questioning actions of yours unrelated to affairs of state . . . The King's authority is a delicate bloom nurtured by the people's faith and esteem, which enable him to reign through the power of his reputation. Once blighted by doubt and criticism, however . . ."

Could Solomon reply that he did not hold the shepherdess captive? She had captivated him, he was in her thrall. Where else among the worldly women of the court could the King find simplicity, or among the devious Daughters of Jerusalem candor? Who matched Shulamith's unadorned beauty and nobility of spirit? Even her devotion to Dod enticed the King

—who loved *him* so passionately yet selflessly? In her artless way Shulamith had become Solomon's teacher. And, he hoped, preserver.

"Well, my lord? What is your decision?"

Solomon arose. "I am going for a ride."

With an attendant's umbrella shading them, the golden-haired charioteer drove Solomon out the eastern Horse Gate. Usually the King rode the city's broad central thoroughfare, with fifty soldiers running ahead to encourage people to admire his royal person while fifty more surrounded his chariot to keep him from being mobbed. Adulation enhanced prestige, he knew, and distance increased adulation. But this time resentment spurred him out a side gate, away from the people. How could these ingrates begrudge him Shulamith? He was mortal, they eternal; long after his reversion to dust, the people would endure within his sumptuous Jerusalem.

"Where to, my lord?"

Someplace the King could muse of things too wonderful for him to understand: the way of an eagle in the air, the way of a ship on the sea, the way of a man with a girl. "My gardens," said Solomon.

Attended by six other chariots, the King's descended the steep limestone ridge into the Valley of Kidron, which sank fifteen miles eastward into the stagnant Sea of Salt. Jerusalem was life; the sea, death; and the wild chaos between, a parable of everyone's journey from birth.

Turning southward, they soon passed the orchard-adorned Spring of Gihon, original source of the city's water supply until Solomon built Jerusalem aqueducts and reservoirs. And to offset its lack of metals, clay, and timber, he imported these, together with foreign artisans skilled in stone, wood and metal work, architects, builders, weavers, dyers, jewelers.

Gods also he imported—to his left now on the wild Mount of Olives, dubbed the Mount of Offense for its alien shrines. His hospitality to his wives and other foreigners, some called corruption. As if the eternal invisible Lord, whom the heavens themselves could not encompass, feared idols of wood and stone, with eyes that saw not, ears that heard not, mouths that spoke not. Others charged the builder of the Lord's own House on the opposite Mount Moriah with love of alien gods. As if what drove men to whoring were not lovelessness.

Palled in smoke to the right now lay the Valley of Hinnom, polluted Gehenna of rotting carcasses

and burning rubbish. Here, despite the lesson of
Isaac's release unharmed from Abraham's binding
on the Temple Mount above, Canaanites still sacrificed their children to Moloch. An example of people
punished not for their sins but by them.

"A race, my lord?"

The ritual question from Solomon's tall, armored
driver. Very long hair sprinkled with the same gold
dust that sparkled his handsome companions, the
charioteer's tunic of Tyrian purple contrasted as painfully with the King's white robe as youth with age.
Another reminder of Shulamith.

"To Etam!" The ritual answer spurred the ritual
responses from the other charioteers, and the race
was on.

How the King loved races. Every month he held
them in his hippodrome; each year a race of ten
thousand was run. Solomon and his court and the
priests and Levites and sages would attend in tunics
of light blue (corresponding to the autumn sky);
other Jerusalemites wore white (winter snow); visit-
ing Israelites, red (summer's ripe fruits); heathens,
green (the Great Sea in the spring). Horse races,
whose losers emerged triumphantly alive, he sometimes preferred to solemn assemblies around the Brazen Altar, where only perfect animals were sacrificed.

His celebration as King of peace had induced him to pursue peacemaking, an instance of a good name determining the man's deeds.

"Here we come, my lord!"

When two chariots overtook Solomon's, he grabbed the reins from the driver to urge on his team. Like suns the gleaming charioteers streaked over hills of olive trees, until the King imagined himself growing wings like the Holy of Holies' cherubim and taking flight. *Here* no longer existed, but only what had to be passed before soon reaching the setting place of the sun.

"Faster! Faster!"

They were magnificent, his Egyptian steeds, bred for beauty and trained for form and speed. Graceful yet strong, all curves and spirit. How proud their bearing, how gallant their nature. So like Shulamith.

Was there nothing that did not remind him of her!

Only the surrounding landscape, an earthly netherworld. Despite the rainy season's legacy of sparse grain and short-lived grass and vivid borages and spring wildflowers of every hue, gray boulders and bald scarps predominated, together with nettles, thorns, and thistles. Life here, amid the brown of scrub and the gray of rock, took the deadly form of marauding lions, wildcats and scorpions.

"Careful, my lord!"

Rounding a turn, the leather-rimmed wooden wheels struck a rock, and Solomon would have bounced from the chariot had his attendant not held him down. When he recovered his balance, Etam had burst forth around the bend to greet him in all its greenery. One more proof of the living God.

Swiftly Solomon passed the leading chariots one by one. Their drivers urged their horses on with words, even as they reined them in. The charioteers always let him win races, and he was ever gracious in victory: ritual concluded.

Separating himself from the others, he wandered alone through flowers and trees he knew by birthdate as well as name, for their growth paralleled his own. Nobody can eat stones, a Northern elder had stated. Wrong. Man is heart as well as stomach, and souls hunger for beauty, and eyes consume gardens, orchards, buildings . . . virgins.

How would the people endure winter without delicate pink almond flowers blossoming from bare branches, when all other trees remain lifeless, assurance of spring eternal and resurrection? And what would women do without the camphire's feathery white henna blossoms, whose dusky-red dye stained their palms and soles and whose leaves provided a yellow stain for hair?

Here was the costly balm, its flowers like tufts of acacia blossoms, a gift from the Queen of Sheba, along with her riddles. Once so rare that soldiers guarded their cultivation, balsams now grew throughout Judah, omnipresent mementos of Solomon's storied black son. There, the twenty-foot almug tree, imported from Ophir together with her gold. Its ruby-colored pilasters of sandalwood perfumed the Temple and Palace, while dyers extracted its rich red hue to color wools—

A sudden idea. By placing streaked branches in their watering troughs, Jacob had caused Laban's flocks to conceive speckled and spotted offspring. Might not flowers similarly brighten Solomon's dreams? God knew they needed light.

For his purpose Solomon searched out a stacte, the perfumed shrub tall as a tree that shimmered with waxy white blossoms like snowdrops. Detaching a cluster of five, he cupped it in his hands and inhaled the fragrance used for incense offerings in the Temple. Then he stared into one flower without blinking until its vivid orange anthers elongated to enfold his body and suck him into the petals. They merged him into their waxen whiteness, as a voice resounded inside his head . . . with words he would rather have died before hearing.

"*. . . because you have not kept My covenant and My statutes, which I have commanded you, I will rend the kingdom from you and give it to your servant. In your lifetime I will not do so, for David your father's sake, but I will rend it from your son. Not all the kingdom, however. I will give one tribe to your son for David's sake. That David may have a lamp always before Me in Jerusalem, the city wherein I have chosen to put My name . . .*"

With all his might Solomon wrung his hands, as Saul should have the neck of the Witch of Endor for divining similar tidings. The stacte remains he mashed into a ball, then raised his arm overhead. But it slipped from his fingers. When he turned around to retrieve it, a ruddy man in white wool stood before him, as if sprung from the stacte. Nightmare's continuation?

Uncertain, the King reached for the sword that was always with him. For royalty attracted assassins; nothing so seductive as power, as doubling one's potency by swallowing another's. "Who are you?"

*Ahijah the prophet.*

A voice like fire—intense, scorching. The voice

of his dream? But Solomon could not tell whether he was yet awake. "Why approach me here, when anyone can see the King in the Hall of Judgment?"

*Solomon sees only people with claims against each other. The prophet's claim is against the King. So Zabud keeps Ahijah away.*

"Nonsense. Zabud is the son of a prophet."

*Rehoboam is the son of Solomon.*

"But Zabud is also my personal priest."

*A priest serves the government; a prophet serves God.*

If this Ahijah actually existed, Solomon could not prevent his talking, for a prophet spoke for the Lord. David had never silenced Nathan. And what did Solomon have to fear? He had never arranged the murder of a husband he cuckolded. "Speak, then."

*A warning. Atop his mount of gold, the King of glitter disports himself as if Israel could never die. He forgets how many times before the Israelites were brought low, once even following Joseph's reign as Egypt's chief minister. But pride still goes before destruction, and arrogance always precedes a fall . . . People will endure hardships so long as their ruler shares them. Nobody will suffer forever in order to support the extravagance of one man and his retinue.*

*Certainly not Israelites, with their history as nomads who scorned the superiority of royalty . . . Does Solomon wish to be remembered for doing to Israel what Samson did to the Philistines?*

"Enough!" Solomon raised his sword and hurled it, then swiftly shut his eyes. He wanted the lies to cease but nobody to die. When he opened his eyes, both wishes had been granted. No further insults, no corpse on the ground . . . no Ahijah. End of nightmare.

If it were but a nightmare.

Upon his return to the capital, Solomon ordered Shulamith brought to the Throne Room. Her eyes would color his dreams better than any flower. And since pleasure was the gift of God, he would make the girl his concubine. How can a man ever be warm alone? Indeed, how can a man alone be anything at all?

Rehoboam was testing the royal chair when Solomon entered. After watching him repeatedly ride it up and down, making love to majesty, the King asked, "Does it fit?"

Rehoboam bolted from the chair and stumbled

down the stairs. "Sitting," he contended with his usual pout, "is the only royal training you've allowed me."

"Sitting, my son, is what you do best."

"And Jeroboam?" He simpered. "What do you think of the sun now, Father? At least the moon never gives anyone sunstroke."

To this smirk the King must leave all, and who knew whether his son would be wise or a fool? Yet he would rule over the kingdom of Israel. Is there a greater evil than a man who has labored with wisdom and skill—all his days pain and nights of no rest—forced to leave everything to one who never labored at all?

His successor would also inherit his concubines, as Solomon did Abishag the Shunemite. And the thought of Rehoboam knowing Shulamith—the King would as soon loose a wild ass in his hyacinth beds.

"My lord." Unnoticed, Shulamith had entered, looking strangely serene for one who had been nearly defiled.

What does an attacker say to his victim? "Good day. How are you?"

"I—I felt better by morning," she stammered.

He sighed. "I felt bested by last night. Will you forgive me?" Could one so young understand that when a man stops loving himself, he's forced to love another? Only her love could replenish his own. "Can you forgive me?"

Rehoboam intervened. "What happened last night, Shulamith?"

She ignored all questions. "About Dod, my lord—"

"Are you demanding his release—and yours?" Solomon asked. "Now if I refuse, you can expose me."

"What did happen, Father?"

"Shulamith, this is your chance."

The girl hesitated.

"Tell me, Shulamith," urged Rehoboam, "and go free."

She bowed her head. "Everyone knows the King is pleased to speak in riddles."

Truly exquisite, this girl, without a blemish. "Enjoyment being the greatest of all commandments, Shulamith, since whoever is happy is fulfilling God's will—" But this was no time for a speech, not when it was her response he wanted to hear. "Shulamith, be my Queen."

Serenity turned to wrath. "Why does everyone mock me!" the girl exclaimed.

"What?" Where was her joy? His thanks?

"First Rehoboam would make me his Queen.

Now the King—who has never married an Israelite."

"The shepherdess is imagining, lying—" Solomon terrorized Rehoboam with a look. "If you must know," the Prince then confessed, "I fell in love with the girl as soon as I saw her." He meant, Solomon knew, the instant the King saw her. "Can I help it, Father, if I am a passionate man? I come by it naturally."

Solomon translated, "It isn't that my son burns to make you Queen, Shulamith, so much as he needs you to make him King. One's latest wife is always his favorite. Why do you suppose Bathsheba bathed entire days on Uriah's roof? A slippery business, the monarchy, and a woman in the right bed often greases the way. Rehoboam fears I shall designate our son my heir."

Rehoboam paled. "You'd never do that, Father!"

"Why not? I come by it naturally. That's how I inherited the throne." He reflected. "Or do I underestimate you? Absalom publicly entered David's concubines on the palace roof in order to establish his right of succession. You remember what happened to him, don't you? And to my other brother, Adonijah, who tried to marry my concubine, Abishag the Shunemite? Rehoboam, anticipation I tolerate—but never acceleration."

Blood rushed to the Prince's face, dissolved his self-control. "No wonder you're *hated!*" he screamed.

"My son, my son, my hateful son." The King could have wept. (After the birth of his firstborn, he had written: Children are a heritage of the Lord; the fruit of the womb is a reward. As arrows in the hand of a mighty man, so are the children of one's youth. Happy is the man that has his quiver full of them; he shall not be put to shame.) Quietly he said, "Better to be hated, my son, than hating."

"Best by far is to be loved and to love!"

That surprised Solomon. "You know of such things?"

"I know you've never given me a chance at either. Some sons may want their fathers dead, but what of fathers who think to prolong themselves by rendering their sons impotent? Yes, you appointed me your successor—but you never let me succeed. David made you joint ruler, while you hoard power. You hoard *yourself*. What do *you* know of love? Of a son who's not a hundredth as able as the father he desperately tries to emulate and can never satisfy?" Rehoboam ran from the room.

Solomon recognized the son described. It was, alas, himself. He had craved his father's love, but David, too, regarded the son of his old age as his supplanter. Nobody shouts "Long live the King" over a king dying. Instead, a Shunemite is prescribed to cradle him to the grave.

Yet since happiness in this futile life is achieved through enjoyment with the woman one loves—the King approached Shulamith. "You see? I don't mock you. Unless you regard marriage to me mockery."

She drew herself up, as impregnable as a rock.

"Like Moses, I assaulted what I should have begged. That sin barred his entry into the Land of Promise. Will you punish me that unmercifully?"

She clasped and unclasped her hands. "My lord has more wives than he can count."

"Yes, I have a great harem. And a greater solitude."

"With all those women to love?"

"You think I'd have so many if I loved any of them? Love never adds, it subtracts. Till there remains but one, Shulamith. Love must be singular. Like God." He caught her hands inside his. "Well?"

Her fingers fluttered like trapped birds. "But my lord is so wise. Me, I'm a sheep."

"Wisdom I don't need, Shulamith. I have enough now to make me unhappy."

"I'd give my *life* for my lord—"

"I want *more*! We all enter this world through

love, so love is the only fitting exodus." Gently he pulled the girl toward him until he could taste her breath. "True, my desire is no less selfish than Rehoboam's. But I offer you what he cannot."

The girl shook her head. "I never wished to be a queen."

"I offer you the love only a hopeless old man can feel for a hopeful young girl." She bowed her head, and her hair caressed his chest. "Will you accept it?"

After a moment Shulamith spoke, with difficulty. "If that's my lord's wish . . . I shall remain in the harem . . . for a while." She intoned each word with equal value, as if matching pearls in a necklace. "Yes, I would like to be your . . . companion."

"That too. Certainly. Or do you mean companion only? The sages have ruled it cruelty to muzzle a bull pastured beside a field of grain."

She nodded.

"What is your decision then?"

"If I only knew . . .!"

"Say you are mine," he implored. "Because without you, Shulamith, this Palace is nothing but an opulent sepulcher. Solomon's pyramid."

Her eyes glistened with tears.

"Are you weeping yes? Tell me. Or are you weeping no?"

She buried her face in her hands and sobbed, "I
can't . . . I can't . . . I can't."

His hands fell away from hers. Life, he thought,
you are a cheat to the end!

Suddenly the doors to the Throne Room were
flung open, and Zabud and the royal guard burst inside. But Solomon was too distracted to pay them
attention, though everyone was shouting as if pursued
by demons. Hundreds of women the King had taken
without desire, only to be spurned now by the one
he craved. Surely old age was the final insult.

". . . Don't you *hear* me, my lord?" The chief
minister was shaking Solomon by the arm. "A mob
has freed the shepherd. Now they're marching on the
Palace itself."

With a start the King recalled his dream in the
gardens at Etam: ". . . because you have not kept My
covenant, I will rend the kingdom from you." And
the encounter that followed with Ahijah the prophet
—perhaps it actually took place. Had Solomon disregarded a messenger of God, with this result?

". . . and I can't tell them the King has already
ordered Dod's release. Nobody would believe it. Now
they want the girl too. If my lord will allow me—you
must make Shulamith your first Israelite wife. That

will pacify the people, especially her being a Northerner."

Solomon shook his head. "I have asked Shulamith to be my Queen—"

The chief minister clapped his hands. "I should know better than to presume to advise the wisest of men."

"—but she rejected me."

*"Impossible!"*

Strange sounds reverberated outside. At first Solomon could not recognize what they were; during his reign he had heard everything except disapproval. He started for the porch, but Zabud blocked his way.

The King gestured toward the middle court. "Don't you hear?" he said wryly. "My people are calling me."

"They might kill you!"

Solomon shrugged, then pushed his chief minister aside. "Hopeless, fearless."

Shulamith ran up to him, pleading, "Stay! Please, my lord. There are so many haters out there."

She didn't want him dead, the King mused, and she didn't want him alive. Only suffering.

"Solomon?" Isis appeared. His bride at the start of his reign attending its possible end. "The last time

I heard such cries," said the Queen, "was our wedding day. Ever since, I have considered noise a good omen."

A pity, he reflected, that a woman who always tendered healing words rarely heard any. He wished to say something to her, to atone for all the years he had said nothing. But now there was no time.

Alone Solomon stepped out on the porch.

A sea of roaring men flooded the court below. Sacrilege so to desecrate his royal compound! But when the human wave swept closer, outrage yielded to a strange yearning. To be overwhelmed beyond memory and desire, all anxieties swamped, drowned, sunk, now that his future was nearly all past, with neither hope nor love to buoy him further.

The royal guard interrupted his perverse reverie by advancing on the people. An armed clash would mean the killing of Israelites, not of him, and the King of peace would be forever stained with blood. Swiftly he ordered his mercenaries to withdraw. Instead they climbed the porch, ringing it with shields of plaited osiers held high.

He recalled David's prayer, "Let me not be put to shame, O Lord, let not my enemies triumph over me." Then, with the mob almost at the foot of the porch, Solomon plunged through the royal guard and shouted with all his might, *"Cease this tumult! Am I the walls of Jericho!"*

That stemmed them. His royal personage still commanded awe. For the moment.

"Impossible to speak to rabble. I don't have a hundred tongues."

"Talk to me then. Their leader."

At first the King could not see the source of this arrogance. Then the crowd parted, like the waters of the Red Sea, to reveal his vicarious son, Jeroboam. Painfully Solomon remembered his words, now twice proven a lie: Happy is the man that has his quiver full of children; he shall not be put to shame.

With Dod at his side, the commander announced, "We've rescued the shepherd from Uriah's fate. Now we demand the girl."

The mob's affirmation came in a single roar. A magician, Jeroboam had transformed hundreds of men into the sea monster Leviathan. Surely its legendary smell, which would render even the Garden of Eden uninhabitable, could be no fiercer than that of this mob spuming sweat.

"There are lawful ways—" Solomon began.

"Lawful, yes—but are they just? Yesterday we petitioned to have our yoke lightened, to enable poor shepherds like Dod to marry." He turned to address Leviathan. "Did Solomon listen?"

The beast growled no, its breath heating the air.

Jeroboam started forward. "Now let's force him!"

Leviathan crouched to spring. The royal guard raised their spears. God in heaven! The first casualties would be forty years of peace.

"*Stop!*" The King threw himself between the two camps. "Stop before you destroy yourselves, and Israel too. Would you be Philistine Samsons!"

The insult froze the beast. For the first time individual voices were raised.

"All we want is the girl."

"Free our sister."

"Free *your* sister."

Still nomads at heart, these people persisted in regarding themselves as a king's brethren and denied unlimited authority. What David had instructed his son, the equality of all Israelites before God, confronted him now. Yet Solomon had no alternative here. "I *can't* release Shulamith," he stated.

"You desire the girl. That's why you won't free her."

How humiliating to confess his need publicly, no different from any commoner's. Dangerous too, for

138

royalty thrived on mystery. "It's true I desire Shulamith. But that's not my reason—"

Leviathan set up a chant, like an antiphonal
rendering of psalms in the Temple court. "He desires
the girl . . . Release the shepherdess . . . We want
the girl . . . Free Shulamith!"

The King demanded attention, then implored it.
"At stake are not my desires, nor the girl, but your
lives. *You* must insist I keep her."

Snorts of laughter.

They were deriding him. Him, Solomon. And
a ruler can survive hatred, but never scorn. "Compel
your King to submit to a mob," he tried to explain,
"and you destroy the monarchy—Israel's strength and
your security. Have you so quickly forgotten the time
of the warrior-judges?"

"We were free then," someone shouted. "Proud,
independent, self-governing tribes—"

"Free! Free for each tribe to be attacked separately. Free to be conquered by every enemy. Free
to depend on occasional warrior-judges for rescue.
Free to live brutishly and briefly. Why did the proud
independent tribes force Samuel the prophet to unite
them under a monarchy, if not to establish peace
through unified rule? Our dream at last fulfilled—
will you smash it and crush Israel!"

139

Gradually Leviathan resumed human form. Then people broke up into small groups to argue the King's words. But where there was argument, there was Jeroboam to override it, descending to the people's level in order to flatter them into thinking themselves on his.

"I've never heard Solomon talk so much. He's frightened! Samuel warned that a king would conscript our daughters and draft our sons, tithe our cattle and produce, and appropriate our possessions—finally enslave us all. Lo the prophecy come true: behold the Pharaoh of Israel!"

Philistine Samson before, now Israelite pharaoh. Solomon's spirit poured out of him like water. "Yes, I am frightened," he conceded, his strength ebbing with each word, "but not for myself. I am an old man; there's little mischief you can do me." Were it done swiftly, he would even welcome its killing the pain that now gripped his chest. "But you as a people are young. If you act foolishly now, you'll destroy Israel forever."

"Words, words, words!" Jeroboam faced the mob, tall and handsome and murderous. *Another* hater. "Here's our chance to uproot the past forty years and start anew!"

A Time for Loving

As if anyone could destroy the past without destroying himself. The past was to build on, to improve, to advance from. Nothing grew on scorched soil, and the only thing chaos ever begot was more chaos. "Heed your King," pleaded Solomon. "Look, I set before you now the blessing and the curse: peace and chaos. Choose peace, if you and your offspring would prosper on this land and not perish. Keep the Law now—"

It was winning them, his appeal to reason, when Dod burst out, "The one who violates the Law now is the King. *You* are the man!"

The prophet Nathan's denunciation of David for stealing Bathsheba, Solomon recalled with pain. And afterward their firstborn had died.

Someone called out, "But the King's reasons are right."

"Of course his reasons are right. Solomon is the shrewdest man in all the world. Yet his deeds are wrong. And isn't that what counts?"

The crowd stirred, confused. Small fights broke out between groups.

"Even Solomon doesn't claim Shulamith's abduction was lawful," Dod continued. "Do you, my lord?"

The King did not reply.

Jeroboam pressed the attack. "Does the Law justify seizing a girl? Can you?"

They leaned forward for the King's answer. He stepped back, unable to say yes, unwilling to say no. "Nevertheless—"

Jeroboam gave chase. "More reasons? Reasons to defy the Law, which is sovereign even over the King?" He beckoned his creation to join in the hunt. "Shall we let our sisters be treated as harlots? Must Solomon defile your wives and daughters before you rise up—?"

The mob slithered forward as one. Leviathan's return.

*"No! Stop!"* Shulamith materialized at the King's side. The beast's roar drowned her out, but her sudden appearance gave it pause.

"Shulamith!" Dod raced to the foot of the porch. When guards intervened with spears, the King ordered them away for fear they would harm him. A mistake, for the girl darted to join her shepherd. Was this what would dispatch the kingdom of Israel—a lovers' embrace?

Jeroboam brandished his sword. "Now to subdue the tyrant and to choose a just King!"

If there were any doubts whom he meant, his cohorts were quick with a suggestion. They chanted

the commander's name like the Levite guild of re-
hearsed musicians.

As the monster surged ahead, the soldiers looked
to Solomon for instruction. He hesitated. How could
a king order an attack on his people? Even animals
did not kill their own.

Suddenly the girl deserted her shepherd. Despite
his pleas, she returned to Solomon. "If my lord will
have me," she shouted, as if the King's life depended
on it, "I would enter his harem."

"Betrayed," cried Dod, "by everyone!" and ran
off.

Shulamith fell to her knees and prostrated herself. The King bent over to help her up, but seeing
her shoulders shaking uncontrollably, let her be.
Women often cry for happiness, he told himself without being convinced.

Meanwhile, Leviathan had fragmented into hundreds of men, now dispersing. In a frenzy Jeroboam
ran about to stay them. Foolish, individuals pointed
out, to rescue a volunteer into Solomon's harem. And
since her lover had departed, what reason for them to
remain?

"Solomon confessed the abduction," Jeroboam
reminded them. "You all heard—"

What abduction? Hadn't the commander heard

Shulamith ask to enter the harem? The first Israelite Solomon had accepted. A Northerner, at that. No injustice had been perpetrated, but an honor.

"What of exorbitant taxes . . . forced labor . . . the King's extravagance?"

But having been instigated to free a prisoner turned queen, the people felt too ashamed to be aroused afresh. And Jeroboam, losing his following, lost himself among them before he could be apprehended. Just as well: the King did not want any of his sons killed, however hateful.

Zabud ran up to the King, and in his jubilation, pounded him on the back. "One man against a mob—and how you triumphed!"

"Another such triumph," Solomon commented, "and you'll be congratulating a corpse."

Shulamith arose unsteadily to her feet, keeping her face bowed.

The King raised her chin. "I think the only prayers God heeds are those offered for others. Shulamith, you are my prayer answered." He wiped the tears from her eyes. "As the Lord lives, I will make you happy."

# SHULAMITH

*Dod was knocking . . .*

*"Let me in, my love. My head is drenched with dew, my hair drips with the mists of the night."*

*"I have disrobed," she replied. "How can I dress ever again?"*

*He withdrew his hand from the opening, and her heart tossed within her.*

*She arose to admit her love, flowing myrrh upon the doorknob. She opened her self to her beloved.*

*But he was gone, vanished.*

*Her soul fled.*

*She ran about the city, through its streets and*

147

*squares. She sought Dod, but could not find him. She
called, but he answered not.*

*The watchmen, on their rounds of the city,
found her.*

*"Have you seen my love?"*

*They struck her, bruised her; the keepers of the
wall stripped her, called her prostitute.*

*"I beg you, O Daughters of Jerusalem! If you
find my love, tell him I am sick with love."*

*They taunted her. "How is your love better than
any other, O fairest of women? What distinguishes
him?"*

*"My love is fair and ruddy, towering above ten
thousand . . . his hair is curly and raven black . . . his
eyes, doves bathing in milk . . . his bearded cheeks,
beds of spices with tendrils of perfume . . . his lips,
lilies trickling myrrh . . . his arms, rounded cylinders
of gold tipped with pink beryl . . . his body, a column
of ivory overlaid with sapphires . . . his legs, pillars
of marble set on golden pedestals . . . He is majestic
as Mount Lebanon, stately as its cedars . . . His mouth
is filled with sweetness . . . All of him is made for
love . . . This is my beloved, O Daughters of Jerusalem . . ."*

Awaking from an evening nap did not end
her dream. Nearby, the harem women were discuss-

ing Shulamith as if she were Delilah come to shave them bald.

"A few bleats from the sheepgirl, and Solomon comes tumbling down."

"We must put her out of our misery."

"Yes, poison."

"Drowning."

Only Rainbow objected. "Forget the sheepgirl. What does she possess that we don't? Merely what Solomon hasn't taken yet. Once he does . . ."

"Of course! The King will discard her then."

"So the sooner the King comes . . ."

". . . the sooner the sheepgirl goes!"

Shulamith fought tears. Dod gone: the mob had presented her with no choice. Soon Solomon: everyone gave her no chance. Her future would be Isis' or Rainbow's: no life. Yet, with an army of Cains menacing Solomon, how could she have stood idly by in the blood of the man of men?

"O fairest of women! Wake up!"

Rousing her, the Daughters of Jerusalem began to prepare the girl anew. She submitted, feeling somebody else were being bathed, perfumed, dressed, bedecked. The virgin offering.

"Now for Solomon's entry," said Rainbow, "and your departure." She rushed her to the door.

Shulamith broke away. "No, not yet! I'm not ready!"

Rainbow winked at the Daughters of Jerusalem, then stretched out her hands and snaked around Shulamith. In a moment others encircled the panicky girl with psalteries and timbrels, dancing and singing.

"O Solomon! Let him kiss me with the kisses of his mouth . . ."

"I drink your kisses up . . ."

"Your caresses are sweeter than wine . . ."

"No wonder every maiden loves you . . ."

"We are happy when you rejoice in us . . ."

"How we love to love you, O Solomon . . ."

"Take me with you, Dod, let's run away . . ."

"For the King has brought me into his chamber, saying . . ."

" 'I shall delight in you, rejoice in your love . . .' "

"O your caresses are sweeter than wine . . ."

"No wonder every maiden loves you . . ."

Shulamith dashed herself against the undulating circle. But the women whirled her from one to the other, swirling her inside a constricting circle of laughter, from queen to concubine to maid, till the room spun and its walls converged upon her.

The girl reeled and fell to the floor. It swayed beneath her. She felt as if she were sliding off.

Somebody steadied her. ". . . your last night here." Gently she was drawn erect. Isis held her. "From now on, you stay with Solomon."

Shulamith recalled Rainbow's words. "For how long?"

A sigh, nearer a lament. "For as long as he lives."

And afterward? Rehoboam would inherit her. She might as well have remained in Shunem and married Mushi.

The Queen braved a smile. "You remind me of my own first night, child. I was as young as you— once. O Shulamith! If the gods had pity, life would be lived backward."

The royal guard entered. To escort Shulamith to the King, she knew, and there was nowhere to hide. Soon the Daughters of Jerusalem pointed the girl out by forming a line straight as an arrow and aiming it at her.

"Not yet!" She threw herself into Isis' arms. "I dream of Dod all the time. I haven't finished grieving for him."

"Finished?" Isis stroked the girl's hair. "I mourn Solomon still."

Shulamith hugged the Queen.

Isis removed her gold collar necklace and placed it around the girl's neck, saying, "It's not a fair exchange, I know. I bequeath you a usek, my child, while you grant me posterity."

The endless reflections of torchlight in the polished bronze vestibule leading to the royal bedchamber blinded Shulamith. She shielded her eyes with her hands, feeling she had stepped into the sun.

"A device to dazzle surprise guests, my reflector vestibule. But you, my love, dazzle *it*."

Her fingers were kissed, then drawn away from her face. Looming before her in bejeweled white linen was the King, like Mount Hermon's snowcap. Only, his damp hands were warm and his cheeks flushed like sunset. Gently he guided her through shadows chasing each other around widely spaced small lamps, an audience of flickering courtiers.

"Shulamith—" His hands reached for her face, stopped at the gold collar.

"Isis gave it to me."

"Of course. She would. The woman of valor all mothers want for their sons. Bathsheba had me memorize her virtues. 'She does her husband good and not evil all the days of her life. She seeks wool and flax, and works willingly with her hands. She rises while it is yet light and gives food to her household, and a

portion to her maidens. She stretches her hands out
to the poor; she reaches forth her hands to the needy.
Strength and dignity are her clothing, and she laughs
at the time to come. She opens her mouth with wisdom, and the law of kindness is on her tongue. She
looks well to the ways of her household and eats not
the bread of idleness . . . Grace is deceitful and beauty
is vain, but a woman of valor that fears the Lord, she
shall be praised.' "

"A woman of valor." Shulamith despaired.
"Everything I am not."

The King smiled. "Good. Me, I always preferred
my mother's example to her advice. Long live grace,
even with deceit, and beauty, however vain; they are
the smiles of life." He seated her on the purple divan.
"Do you know, Shulamith? We are the same age as
David and Bathsheba when *they* met."

For a moment the girl envisioned a son of hers
the ruler over Israel and beyond. The seed of David
and Solomon, he would be the king of kings and she
the mother of kings. Of course, only one name would
do for her firstborn: Dod.

Solomon took her hand and rubbed it. "Will you
unclench, my love? It's difficult to hold fists."

She straightened her fingers, and he kissed palms
wetter than the Jordan.

"Wine?" He gave her a gold cup, which she proceeded to spill. The second cup he spilled himself. Could the King, whose days on earth were nothing but first nights, also be nervous?

"Later, my lord. Afterward." Let it be over, done, something no longer to anticipate, nor to be feared. Yet now he wanted to talk. Probably to postpone. What could succeed desire fulfilled but disappointment?

"I am in your debt, Shulamith. For changing me into the resurrection plant." A plant, he explained, that withers into a skeletonlike ball during the dry season and blows across the barren plains of the Sea of Salt. But it takes root again as soon as it rests in moisture; then its stems uncurl, leaves turn green, flowers bloom, and the dead ball stretches out flat and alive once more on the face of the earth. "Shulamith, you have quickened me!"

Indeed Solomon's eyes shone brighter, skin rosier, hair and beard darker. His movements were jaunty, as awkwardly excited as a youth entering his first wife.

"Shulamith. For you I have jeopardized my reign, but I can't regret it. Every man is impelled to love twice in a lifetime—at the beginning, when he wants to share future triumphs; and at the end, to cushion life's ultimate defeat. Do you understand?"

Joys shared doubled, she believed, while sorrows shared mysteriously halved. But the time to love, wasn't that always?

"No matter. I want loving, not understanding." His lips sank into the hollow of her throat.

The journey of her dreams since meeting Dod she was now beginning alone. Yet her faithless body reacted to the King's caresses as to Dod's. Shamefully she felt herself flowing toward them in welcome, inviting more. When his knee inserted itself between her legs, she heard doors burst apart and a sudden rush of wind pierced her.

Solomon mounted her.

But then, *another*. Dod?

Now both rolled over her together . . . separately . . . squeezing . . . grasping . . . stabbing at her . . . All at once he . . . they . . . slid away . . . thudded to the floor.

She opened her eyes. *"Lord!"*

Before the now frenzied shades, a white shadow grappled one black as a piece of night broken off. Swords gleaming, Solomon and Dod tried to sheathe them in each other's belly.

*"Don't kill him! Please don't kill him!"*

155

The King had the advantage of not being blinded by the vestibule of polished bronze. Presently one sword clattered to the floor. Not Solomon's. His forced itself down on the black other, until he went limp.

"How often I wished you were born my son, Jeroboam. Instead"—the King's voice broke—"you are David's son. A second Absalom."

Praise God! It was *not* Dod.

Two Israelites ran into the room with swords held high. The same pair who had helped the royal guard capture Shulamith and Dod the night before. Before they could spring to the King's aid, the men, too, were momentarily blinded by the vestibule's reflections.

"This time," cried Jeroboam, "the triumph is Absalom's!"

"You think so?" Solomon dug his sword into the commander's throat. "Invite your men to leave, or—"

*Jeroboam's* men? (Betrayed, Dod had cried before, by *everyone*.)

The assailants paused. Jeroboam ordered them to attack.

As they slowly advanced, Solomon pricked his captive's skin, saying, "You hope to be King, Jeroboam, but remember, only the living can hope. Even a live dog is better than a dead lion. The living know at least they'll die, but what do the dead know? Even the memory of them dies. Their loves, their hates, their passions, all perish—no longer do they share in anything that goes on under the sun."

"You can't frighten me! I'm not afraid of death!"

"No? Then you're braver than I." Solomon's sword drew blood.

"Stop! Don't—!" His men halted.

"Now," commanded the King, "dismiss them."

"When you free me."

"Ask me something less foolish, like beheading myself."

"Should my men leave without me, I am dead."

"I shan't have your blood on my hands, Jeroboam. You have my word."

"Then you'll imprison me forever."

"You'll not languish in prison. I vow that too."

"How do I know you'll keep your word?"

"You will have to trust me." Solomon grimaced. "As I always trusted you."

Reluctantly Jeroboam ordered his men away. They retreated into the vestibule's blaze of light, where they disappeared as if consumed.

Moments later the royal guard appeared in the

same bronze enclosure. They took charge of Jeroboam, already demanding to be released. Solomon, he declared, had guaranteed his freedom.

The King confronted Jeroboam. "The man you were, I loved. The assassin you've become—" To the guards: "Execute him in the morning."

The commander blanched. "Your vow—"

"You committed suicide," Solomon stated. "By killing me, as you still plan, you would invite all would-be-kings in the land to kill you—and there'd be thousands if you succeeded. So I am only anticipating your death at your own hand."

The guards hurried Jeroboam to the door. There he rallied. "Nobody can execute me. God will not permit it," he cried. "I shall be the next King over Israel. So the Lord has decreed."

That amused Solomon. "Everyone speaks in God's name on state occasions—nations in wartime, rulers at anointments, murderers at regicide. Nothing is so welcome as divine instruction, especially when it sanctions one's ambitions."

"My lord, ever hear of Ahijah the prophet?" the commander asked. "Last week he rent his cloak into twelve pieces and handed me ten, as a sign that God would rend the ten Northern tribes from you and give them to me."

"Ahijah!" The name struck Solomon down. He slumped into a chair. "If there is an Ahijah who prophesied as you say, why did you come yesterday to ask me to lighten the people's yoke? Why?" The King straightened up. "Of course! You came to provoke me into rejecting the Northern petition. In order to incite support for yourself."

"That's not so—"

"And Dod you *wanted* imprisoned. Better yet, killed. To outrage the people further—"

Jeroboam could no longer contain his pride. "Solomon the wise! I've outwitted you twice, and I'll do it again!"

"As the Lord lives!" The King jumped to his feet. "Why, you're no more concerned for the people than—"

"—than *you* are!"

The two glared at each other, their eyes shouting accusations and refuting them.

Solomon was the first to wilt. Bowing his head, he said, "Some difference between us. You burn to become King, and I yearn to stay King."

The commander bowed low. "You are my teacher, I am your pupil. And you cannot execute someone so like yourself, my lord."

With a firm step Solomon strode to his attacker.

"My enemies I can forgive. David taught me that, magnanimity to foes. Despite all his opportunities to kill Saul, who sought his death, my father never grasped one . . ."

Jeroboam smiled and shook off his captors' grip.

"But I can never forgive friends." Solomon's voice wavered as he addressed the guards. "Away with him."

"My lord! My lord!"

"I advise you," said the King, "to address all your future petitions to *my* Lord."


They sat in silence, each feeding on his own thoughts, as slaves carried away the same amounts of food they had served.

Don't kill him, Shulamith had cried before. Which one had she implored, and whom wished spared? Impossible to decide. Easier to choose her own death than between the lives of two she loved.

She loved Solomon? The sudden knowledge startled her. How could she love two men at the same time? Enemies! Still, the King and the shepherd shared the common fate: both were strangers and sojourners before God, their days on earth like a shadow, with no hope of abiding. In the meantime, nobody under the sun was as powerful, glorious, triumphant, majestic as Solomon—or more in love with her. And love had evoked love: his near-murder made her realize that.

Wine finally loosened the King's tongue. After draining his third wineskin, he addressed himself. "Had I been killed, what would I be remembered for? For slaking my lust with a thousand wives, of course —with the thousand wives I never had. If there's one thing people believe, it's that everyone else enjoys more lovemaking than they."

Hesitantly Shulamith spoke up. "The Temple of the Lord. Surely that will live longer than history."

Solomon shook his head. "That imitation of the royal chapels of foreign rulers, even to the sphinxes inside its Holy of Holies? Unlikely. It was designed to make Jerusalem the religious center of all the tribes, North and South. But to confine God, the Creator of all, to a House built with human hands is to controvert His nature. Rulers may need unifying symbols and people may want temples, but the Lord requires hearts." He poured himself more wine. "No, like everyone else I'll be forgotten too. What the earth swallows up, nobody remembers."

"Solomon's wisdom, then. It will outlast memory itself."

"What wisdom? Since the beginning of wisdom is the fear of the Lord, I have been a fool. And one fool can destroy much good, as a single dying fly putrifies the finest perfume. Perhaps every folly, being the child of all past ones, is pardonable. But who can forgive any folly for fathering so many future follies?" He bowed his head. "Not I."

"So harsh a judgment." Her heart going out to him, she tried to smooth away the pain that creased his brow.

Solomon looked up, grateful. "Do *you* forgive me? Can you, perhaps, love me?" He caught her hand, gripped it. "Shulamith, you don't realize. When you're young, it's impossible *not* to be in love. But at my age, it's the supreme act of creation . . . the only one remaining . . . rebirth. Shulamith, love me that I may begin all over again. You must! Love me, Shulamith, for all those who don't."

She took a deep breath. "Yes, my lord. I will." She stroked his hand, which was smooth as beaten gold. "I already do," she whispered, so softly the King may not have heard.

"Love!" He pushed aside the table and drew her to bed, a replica of the jeweled throne stretched flat and wide. "Love is strong as death, passion as unyielding as the grave. The flames of love are flames of fire, a blaze kindled by God. Floods cannot quench love, rivers cannot drown it. Yet if a man gave up his kingdom for love, everyone would despise him." He pulled her down beside him. "Shulamith, love is *you*." He reached out for her.

Instinctively she folded her arms.

His hand glided down and removed her sandals. "Such graceful feet." Tenderly he disrobed her.

"*Oh* . . ." A tremor rippled through her limbs. Her breathing quickened.

"O Shulamith . . . The roundings of your thighs are like jewels, the work of a craftsman . . . Your navel is a rounded goblet, full of aromatic wine . . . Your belly, a mound of wheat, hedged round with lilies . . ."

Lord! The voice was Solomon's, but the mouth was Dod. And when the King spoke, she heard Dod too, alternating with him. Her arms opened wide.

"Your breasts are two fawns . . ."

"*. . . breasts are two gazelles . . .*"

"Your eyes are the pools of Heshbon . . ."

"*. . . eyes like doves . . . teeth, newly shorn sheep . . .*"

". . . hair like threads of royal purple . . ."

"*. . . hair as black as the goats that trail down Mount Gilead . . .*"

". . . and a King is bound captive in its tresses . . ."

163

"... *Honey and milk are under your tongue ...*"
"O love, how beautiful, how sweet you are ..."
"*I lick honey from your comb ...*"
"... and all for voluptuous delights ..."

His lips grazed every part of her. She felt herself dissolving in waves of flame.

"Your bearing is like a palm tree . . . your breasts like clusters of grapes . . . Let me climb up into that palm tree . . . and take hold of its branches . . ."

A deep flush spread downward to her uncurling toes . . . Her breasts swelled within his hands . . . The nipples stood erect over a heart beating wildly enough to topple them . . .

"Your mouth is the choicest wine . . ."
"*... lips like bands of scarlet ...*"
"... that glides down sweetly ..."
"*... mouth so comely ...*"
"... exciting the lips of this eager lover ..."

Finally the two voices merged, Solomon and Dod became one as she enveloped, then embodied him. Her twin love.

"*I am come into my garden!*"

Her body contracted and expanded, then contracted again, as if giving birth. To herself, it seemed, for she was turning inside out. She cried out again and again, unable to stop. But as she tried to catch her breath, her soul sank . . . dropped . . . hurtled down. She felt suddenly bereft. Widowed so soon?

When she opened her eyes, nobody lay beside her. Her lover had vanished. She was alone. Another dream?

"Go, Shulamith." Solomon stood at a window far across the room.

She covered herself. "My lord?"

"One doesn't expect to be addressed as King over Israel while making love," he said. "But I will not be called Dod."

*Oh . . . !*

"Go home, Shulamith. Love must be given; it cannot be exacted. A woman is not won who must be forced."

"But I came willingly."

"Pity is a mighty lever. As mighty as a mob."

"Not pity, never pity. Affection . . . reverence . . . love."

"Impossible." He stared out the window as if surveying his past. "I have never been loved. David was loved. Solomon is admired."

She went to him. "Admiration, love: what difference is there? Both mean someone cares whether you live or—" She broke off.

"A fatal distinction. Love consecrates; admira-

165

tion inflates. My father shared the burdens of the people, while I multiply them. Is it any wonder! I was born to the purple, to an ambitious mother who conspired to get me the throne—and she succeeded." He threw up his hands. "See how a great man accepts his failure? He blames it on a woman."

"Failure? My lord's ideals and all—"

"We speak ideals and speak them, Shulamith, and never grow up to them. While I ruled Israel, what ruled me? Power and pleasure, splendor and fame. Yes, I made this land a light to the world. But a kingdom with few resources, buildings, commerce, established ways cannot be made the world's greatest nation in one generation." A grimace. "Jeroboam taught me something too: nobody should ascend to power who craves it; he wants it for his own purposes, not his nation's. Look how I gutted my own people. God forgive me!" He turned away. "Go, marry the one you love. While I right my kingdom. Your jewelry is your bride-price."

Incredibly, she heard herself say, "I don't want to leave you."

"Human sacrifice ended in Israel with Abraham and Isaac."

"No sacrifice. I love my lord also."

"Am I an addition then? A king is used to being all, first and last."

"But you are! *Both* of you are." How to explain her feeling that Dod was the young Solomon, and Solomon the aging Dod? Two profiles of the same face, divided by time. "To love more than one man—is that sinful?"

"Yesterday I thought so"—the King's face softened—"but not now, not after your giving up Dod to save me. Now I see that love is like the moon: if it doesn't wax, it wanes. Truly loving somebody enables one—*compels* one—to love others." He smoothed the hair away from her face and stroked it. "I can't repay evil for good, Shulamith. What would befall you if I died before a son of ours was old enough to ascend the throne and protect you from Rehoboam? Better that you marry a youth who won't leave you a young widow. If the sacrifices of the Lord are a broken heart, better it not be yours. So many years lie in wait for you now, you shall need a heart that's whole." Wryly he exclaimed, "Something new under the sun! Solomon chooses another's future over his own present." He looked startled, as if he had accidentally solved the riddle of riddles. "Perhaps *that* is love."

Shulamith yearned to stay, for surely the King needed her more than Dod did. But most of all now, she felt, Solomon needed to offer up a sacrifice, and it would be heartless to reject it. Sometimes the law of lovingkindness required the acceptance of an unwanted gift. When her father strove to ease her grief over his impending death, she had smiled him to sleep every night, then wept alone till dawn. "If that is your wish, my lord, that I leave—"

"My wish? I wish—" A sigh like a sirocco. "But the time has come, Shulamith, for me to let you go. Everything has its appointed time, for every pursuit there is a season . . . There's a time to be born, and a time to die. A time to plant, and a time to uproot. A time to kill, and a time to heal. A time to wreck, and a time to build. A time to weep, and a time to laugh. A time to mourn, and a time to dance. A time to love . . . and a time to . . ." His voice faded away.

Tears filled her eyes. She had loved two men in her life, and made both unhappy.

"Come, Shulamith, banish sadness from your heart, for youth is a fleeting breath." He cradled her face in his hands. "This is what I have discovered: it's good to eat and drink and enjoy the results of one's toil during your scant years, for it's God who provides the joy in one's heart. So whatever you're able to do, do while you can with all your might, for nothing is done in the grave. Rejoice then in your youth, and follow the impulses of your heart and the desire of your eyes. Only know that in the end God will call you to account. As I am called now. Meanwhile, throughout the fleeting days granted you under the sun, enjoy happiness with the one you love. That is life's reward."

Shulamith retrieved her tunic. But after donning it, she grew afraid. What if nobody wanted her? "How can I ever explain to Dod—?"

"Anyone who has you won't require an explanation also. No man could be that greedy."

"And how explain to my lord? Bathsheba was right to warn. I deceived you—your hopes—"

Solomon went to her. "Nobody ever deceives us, Shulamith; we always deceive ourselves. I should have realized from the start I would never know you. David never knew Abishag the Shunemite, and God always repeats what was. The Lord's way of teaching people who never want to learn." He forced a smile. "Go your way then, eat your bread with joy, and drink your wine with a glad heart. God has already approved your actions."

She embraced him. "My lord? Forgive me."

"For what? For being young? Youth calls to youth. It was foolish to expect you to cure me of old age." He shrugged. "Life is a habit like any other; it's difficult to break. But one can sink in the quicksands of time with beauty and grace if he recalls that nothing ever lives up to expectations, so why should death?"

"Solomon will live!" Shulamith vowed. "He will never die so long as Israel and I have any memory."

Tenderly he kissed her, lingering at her lips. Then he sent her away to Shunem, and to Dod.

# SOLOMON

No more nightmares.

That night the King did not dream. He was too busy to fall asleep. A multitude of plans crowded his mind. With Shulamith gone, only Israel remained for Solomon to rejoice. So many ideas to carry out now, so many projects to fit into too little future. But first to drive away the visions of someone else delighting in Shulamith.

Jealousy was as cruel as the grave! For not only did he envy Dod. All of Solomon's toil and skill: nothing but rivalry with a shepherd gone forty years. Surely this was the greatest vanity of all, trying to outshine his dead father with highways and chariot cities and the most magnificent of royal courts when he should have been shepherding men and women and children. Would Solomon's extravagance cost Israel what the pyramids cost Egypt? Bankruptcy had forced the pharaoh to surrender his daughter to a descendant of Egyptian slaves. Had Solomon, lusting after glory, sacrificed his people to his pretensions?

The Lord had promised to establish the House of David on Israel's throne so long as its descendants walked before Him. How far had Solomon strayed from integrity and uprightness? Would God now cut him off forever because of his transgressions? A riddle worthy of Solomon: how could one who had started his reign with all the answers conclude it with questions only?

The King could wait no longer. Before morning he summoned Zabud to announce revisions in his policies of taxation and conscription, and the appointment of Rehoboam as co-regent.

The chief minister responded, "Long live Solomon! As long as Methusaleh."

Further, the King ordered Jeroboam set free.

"*Before* he's executed?"

"Executions are as good for a ruler as funerals for a physician."

"Jeroboam plots to overthrow you—*kill* you."

"Ever behead a worm, Zabud? It doesn't help. The only rebels I can execute are those whose charges are so false the people won't follow them. And such rebels are too harmless to execute."

"Everyone will think Ahijah's prophecy has frightened you—"

"It has! Doesn't it frighten you?"

"Certainly not. Our mercenaries can always force the people—"

"And then keep reinforcing the force? Thereby spawn future rebellions? Trust not in oppression, Zabud. The question isn't whether I have the power to make the people wretched, but whether it's not in my interest to make them happy. A nation is not ruled when it must be constantly subdued—as with a woman. Government is a marriage, a covenant."

"But freeing a would-be regicide—"

"What better way to announce that I am no longer set in my loose ways, that I am changing in order to keep Israel stable? Anyone can make mistakes, but only a fool persists in them." Indeed the change had already started: Zabud was disagreeing with him. Or he with Zabud. That disturbed him: who during all these years had absorbed whom?

At dawn Solomon set off alone to make the Lord a belated gift of his remaining days on earth.

Do all men give themselves to God, he wondered, when young girls quit them?

Outside, the dome of night was lifting. Soon the sun would strike from Moab's opalescent hills across the desert, glancing off the Mount of Olives with its host of foreign shrines. Why the need to ingratiate himself with all peoples and gods except his own? Why value them more than himself?

Chasing after wind!

His ascent of the Temple Mount ended more slowly than it began; the stairway, instead of his days, had lengthened. At the top he had to rest. Turning around to appraise the massive compound below, he now saw how walled away it was, like his life, from the people whose labor had fashioned it. Half his reign constructing the buildings in this area alone, twenty years that should have been invested in Israelites.

*"My people, my people, why did I forsake you!"*

At the Molten Sea he was flooded with memories of his ablutions on that day of days, the dedication of the Temple. (Odd, how clearly he could recall what happened thirty years before, but not events of the last week—as if youth were reality and old age, vapor.)

His father had led the Holy Ark into the City

of David, shamelessly leaping and dancing and shouting half naked before the Lord. A subscriber rather
than a believer, Solomon had transferred the Ark
with dignity to its permanent home on the Temple
Mount. The elders of Israel, Levite choirs and Temple musicians, also Israelites from all over the land
as well as foreigners, followed the stately procession
of priests. They bore the Ark, nothing in it save the
two tables of stone placed there by Moses when the
Lord covenanted with the Israelites at the time of the
exodus from Egypt. To the accompaniment of one
hundred and twenty priestly trumpets and singers
praising the Lord's goodness and mercy, the Ark of
the Covenant was deposited beneath the wings of the
cherubim inside the windowless Holy of Holies.
Then a cloud filled the Temple with God's glory,
and everyone prostrated himself.

The twenty-six-year-old monarch had reflected
aloud: "The Lord said He would dwell in thick darkness. So I built You a House of habitation, a place
for You to dwell in forever. But will God dwell on
earth? The heavens cannot contain You; how much
less this House that I have built!"

Before the Brazen Altar, Solomon had mounted
a platform erected for the occasion and blessed the
congregation of Israel, then said, "David my father

177

yearned to build a House for the Ark of the Lord's Covenant and for the footstool of our God. But when he started preparations, the Lord told him, 'You shall not build a House for My name, because you are a man of war and have shed blood. Your son Solomon, a man of peace, shall build My House, for I have chosen him to be to Me for a son, and I will be to him a Father.' "

Having implied that he was David's superior, which for the rest of his life he would try to establish, Solomon knelt and spread out his hands toward heaven. Acting as chief priest, he prayed, "Hearken to the supplication of Your servant and of Your people Israel when they pray toward this place. And when You hear, forgive . . . If they sin against You—for there is no man that sins not—and if they say, 'We have sinned, we have done iniquitously, we have done wickedly,' if they return to You with all their heart and with all their soul . . . then hear their supplication and forgive Your people and grant them compassion. For they are Your people, Your inheritance . . .

"O Lord God, never turn away from the face of Your anointed; remember the good deeds of David Your servant."

Clever, thought the old Solomon of the young Solomon, to begin by diminishing his father to the people, then to close by reminding God, who knew better, of David's merit.

Presently a dream brought the Lord's response. "I have heard your prayer and have hallowed this House. My eyes and My heart shall be there perpetually," God said. "If you will walk before Me, as David your father walked, in integrity of heart and uprightness, then will I establish the throne of your kingdom over Israel forever, as I covenanted with David your father. But if you turn away from following Me, you or your descendants, and forsake my commandments and worship other gods, then will I pluck Israel up by the roots out of the land which I have given them. This House will I cast out of my sight, and Israel shall be a byword and epithet among all peoples."

Now Solomon covered his face with his hands and wept. *"O Lord, my God, I abandoned You too!"*

Clearly, the King had outwitted himself. To thwart prophets of the One God, like Samuel and Nathan who denounced Israel's first two kings, Solomon had encouraged the worship of foreign deities. So well did this submerge the Lord's prophets in a sea of pagan gods that no prophet save Ahijah had arisen during his reign. But with no prophet to criticize Solomon continually, he had succeeded in misleading his kingdom. Foolish Rehoboam was right: a ruler can be too strong for his people's good—and his own too. Alas! Man was created plain, but Solomon had sought out too many solutions.

Yet why, during the thirty-year interval, why hadn't the Lord Himself again appeared to warn the King? Or had Zabud barred Him also? Now, Ahijah's prophecy of dissolution. Was it Solomon's wish to take the nation with him in death? A Philistine Samson indeed.

Solomon hurried up the ten stairs to the Temple. To catch his breath he paused between the two dizzyingly high bronze pillars, another reminder of Samson. It sent him rushing through the Temple's open portico to the carved set of doors at the rear, whose gold inlay mirroring the dawn made it seem the sun was rising inside.

The sanctuary doors opened on fluttering whitenesses, like birds of snow. They startled him, priests in white robes tending the golden candlesticks, table of showbread and altar of incense. At Solomon's command, they vanished in reverential silence, closing the doors behind them and entrapping the murk.

Scant light pierced the small latticed windows beneath the ceiling, and the gold-inlaid walls emanated the eerie dimness of the netherworld. Dread clutched his heart, squeezed it. Perspiring and chilled, he searched the sanctuary for pilasters of carved palm trees, the trees of life. But gloom shrouded them from view. Soon sweet-smoking incense choked him, and terror clawed his chest. He was suffocating.

*"O Lord! I walk through the valley of the shadow of death—and I fear."*

The King fled toward the awesome chamber ahead. If the sacrifices of God were a contrite spirit, surely the Lord would now deliver Solomon from all his fears and redeem his soul.

More steps? The top this time must be the heavens themselves. His hands slippery with sweat, he flung open the door to the Holy of Holies.

Only then did he remember that the Lord's throne room was a windowless cube of blackness. God had set the sun in the heavens, but Himself decreed to dwell in thick darkness. No light at all here, save for what filtered through the doorway.

Twin fifteen-foot cherubim—lions with human heads, made of olive wood overlaid with gold—spanned the chamber with their wings. Outer wings touching the Temple walls, and inner ones, each other, the cherubim enthroned God's presence. Beneath their joined wingtips lay the stone tables of the Law inside the Ark, a gold-plated box of acacia, the wood of immortality.

That was all the cubed chamber contained, nothing more. No images of the Divine, as in all other temples, though foreigners believed the Holy of Holies stabled replicas of a divine menagerie: a bull, a pig, a snake, the head of an ass. Yet how condemn aliens for not discerning that the valuables of life are invisible, when Solomon himself needed reminding?

The airlessness of the Holy of Holies oppressed him. Nothing there to breathe but blackness. Gasping, he prostrated himself before the Ark to ask forgiveness. When David had repented his adultery and Uriah's murder, God granted him nearly a score of years more.

Alas! No words came to Solomon now, nor could any be summoned. How did a man resume talking to One he had disregarded for decades? Strive as he did, the King could not attain prayer. His old words of supplication, like his ability to love before meeting Shulamith, had withered from disuse. When a man had everything, what was there to pray for?

*"O Lord! Teach me how to pray."*

The King recalled Moses pleading to be allowed to lead his people to the other side of the Jordan, being spurned, yet telling the Israelites that whenever they search for God they will find Him, if only they seek

Him with all their heart and soul. For the Lord is a compassionate God.

Surely, then, He would reward Solomon at this time for transforming Jerusalem into the heart of the world, its Temple the focus of all prayers and hopes. The King may have overtaxed the resources of his people, but just as pruning renews a tree's branches and hair grows more quickly for being cut, so the Land of Israel had prospered beyond measure. Soon more fruits would grow, ones the Israelites would be allowed to keep, while Jerusalem would abide forever as the capital of the world, the shrine of mankind.

Suddenly Solomon's head filled with a rush of sound. It seemed giant wings were reaching down for him. The cherubim? Their task in the Garden of Eden, he recalled, was to bar trespassers from the Tree of Life. Or were those the wings that had beat down on the Egyptian firstborn?

All thought of prayer fled. Now Solomon could only beg, *Pass over! Angel of Death, pass over me!*

His face felt wet. Blood to smear on the doorposts? Wiping at his eyes, he remembered the resurrection plant. All it needed to come alive was moisture —and here it was. Tears. Surely there were gates in heaven that opened to prayers of brine.

Indeed he revived. Swift bursts of energy shot through him. He straightened up and propelled himself upright. Buoyant now, he felt himself in another race. No matter how far behind he had fallen, it would once more end in his victory. Solomon the King willed it!

"What will it profit You, O Lord, my going down to the grave? Can the dust praise You? Shall it declare Your truth?" he shouted. "I concede God's omnipotence and my own mortality. But You cannot set my sun while it is yet day! I have so much to undo!"

Too taxing for his soul, the battle against fright now happily won. The floor was slithering away. Thick darkness encompassed him . . . His spirit failed.

Was he no resurrection plant, after all, but an ancient olive tree? It always sent up a new young shoot just before crashing to earth . . .


"Too late . . ." God's response?
"Finally . . . ! At last . . . !" Rehoboam, of course.
"Too late . . ." His people?
"Solomon! Wait for me . . . !" Isis. Dear Isis.
"Too late . . ." The physician.
"*Long* . . ."
Astride David's mule, a fifteen-year-old boy rode

up to be anointed ruler over all Israel to the sound of the ram's horn, flutes, the people's joyous shouts of *Long live King Solomon!* And the youth, frightened for all his precociousness, prayed for an understanding heart to enable him to discern between good and evil.

"... *live* ..."

A couple appeared. David and Bathsheba. After so many years. All his life he had yearned to be reunited with them. Had he disappointed them? Were they welcoming him? Bathsheba and David, his first loves.

"... *the* ..."

Where was his dark but exquisite last love? ... The flames of love are flames of fire, a blaze kindled by the Lord . . . Suddenly warm lips pressed down upon his, fiercely insistent. Shulamith? Shulamith!

"... *King!*"

The time for loving . . . was. And yet Solomon lunged upward with all his heart even as he felt his soul drawn from his body by a kiss.

*S*o Solomon slept with his fathers and was buried in the City of David. And Rehoboam his son became King in his stead.

When Jeroboam heard of the death of Solomon, he returned from Egypt, where he had fled. Jeroboam and all the congregation of Israel came and spoke to Rehoboam, saying, "Lighten the hard service and heavy yoke that your father placed upon us, and we will serve you."

The King consulted with his father's advisers, who told him, "If you will now be kind to this people, serve them and be attentive to them, then will they be your servants for all time."

But Rehoboam forsook the elders' counsel and instead answered the people harshly: "I will even add to your yoke! My little finger, remember, is thicker than my father's loins."

So Israel rebelled against the House of David and made Jeroboam King. None followed the House of David but the tribes of Judah and Benjamin. And there were wars between Rehoboam and Jeroboam continually . . .

Then Jeroboam said in his heart: "This Northern kingdom may yet return to the House of David. If this people go up to offer sacrifices in the House of the Lord at Jerusalem, their hearts may turn back to Rehoboam, King of Judah, and they might kill me and return to him." Thereupon Jeroboam made two calves of gold, and told his people, "You have ascended long enough to Jerusalem. Behold your gods, O Israel, which brought you up out of the land of Egypt." And he set the one in Beth-el and the other in Dan . . .

Rehoboam dwelt in Jerusalem and built cities for defense and fortified Judah's strongholds. But when the kingdom of Rehoboam was established and he was strong, he forsook the Law of the Lord, and his people with him . . . So in the fifth year of Rehoboam's reign, King Shishak of Egypt attacked Jerusalem. He captured Judah's fortified cities and entered Jerusalem and took away all the treasures of the House of the Lord and the treasures of the King's house. The Pharaoh carried off everything which Solomon had wrought.

*About the Author*

A native New Yorker, HERBERT TARR is a graduate of Brooklyn College, Herzliah Teachers College, Columbia University and Hebrew Union College-Jewish Institute of Religion. He holds degrees in English (magna cum laude, Phi Beta Kappa), Education, Comparative Literature (with honors) and two in Hebrew Letters. His earlier novels are *The Conversion of Chaplain Cohen* and *Heaven Help Us!*